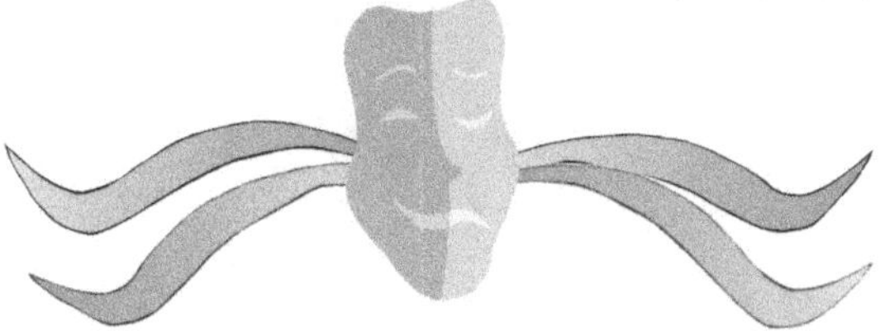

Day 20 of our journey

So, today Amanita was in a total grump and everyone tried to avoid her while we rode along what someone has finally explained is called the 'Tea Road.' Apparently, that's the name because the best tea is grown in that Darjil place where Valderon Raven'sWing enchanted the whole populace, and then it's transported up here for sale around the world.

Getting hold of a map has been nearly as hard as getting hold of a calendar.

And, honestly, I could probably just ask, and someone would show me one or explain, or something. But there hasn't been much of an opportunity to ask anyone. Commander Zaja likes it quiet at meals, and nobody goes against her. And I really want to see this stuff written down, so asking while we're riding is probably not a good idea; I haven't tried reading while riding yet, but my stomach gets tickly in a bad way, just thinking about it.

Though Puck does it all the time, since Chillabiaen doesn't need direction any more than Twinklestar does.

Hunh. Which means if I could get over my guts, I could probably do it.

Anyways, I'm going to try talking to Daffyd in a few minutes. If we whisper, maybe I can get some more details of what's going on out of him. He seems to know what's going on, but when he tried to explain last night, we got those girl-guards pounding on the door and telling us to 'quiet down.'

Nanny-goats, all of them.

Diary of a ~~Runaway Prince~~ Bold Questing Hero

Book Five of the Prankster Prince

(Book One of the Pathremiri Problem)

Mangala McNamara

Rising Dragon Books

Also available in eBook and paperback editions.
McNamara, Kerridwen Mangala
Diary of a ~~Runaway Prince~~ Bold Questing Hero by Mangala McNamara Indiana: Rising Dragon Books, 2024
 154p. 1 map
(McNamara, Mangala. The Prankster Prince; bk. 5)
Summary: Prince Thony and his friends have saved all the worlds in the universe – now he needs to get back to his Bold Quest to find a princess to marry (with a wealthy and powerful father so he can bring troops back home to save his land. But first he has to visit Amanita's homeland… where they don't like guys too much

ISBN 978-1-960160-53-9 (pbk)
1. Princes and princesses - Fiction. 2. Adolescent Rebellion - Fiction
ISBN 978-1-960160-54-6 (hc) ISBN 978-1-960160-49-2 (eBook)

ISBN: 978-1-960160-53-9
First Print Edition: October 2024
10 9 8 7 6 5 4 3 2 1

For my son Rhodri, who actually falls on the floor
laughing when I read these books to him.

And for all the rest of my kids – whose weird obsessions
with *Diary of an 8-Bit Warrior* and *The Dork Diaries*
inspired this book.
(Okay, fine, I read most of them, too.)

CONTENTS

THONY
and the Much-Anticipated
Adventure
Book One
of the
Prankster Prince
MANGALA MCNAMARA

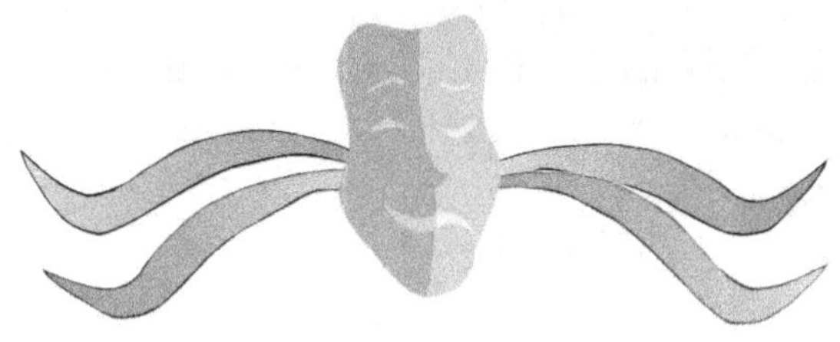

Okay,
this is SUPER lame.

Just because Amanita and I were talking about how incredibly *flat* and *boring* this place is, that Commander Zaja is forcing us to write it down instead of talk about it.

I mean, she was nice about it and everything.

I guess.

She had us all stop early for the night and went out into the market of the dinky little town *(I mean, it's more like the villages at home than Flowerdust, and they all keep telling me* **that** *was a small town)* and bought these little books of blank paper.

(And seriously? Can it really be that small a place if they have **paper** *and* **books** *for sale on the* **street***?)*

Oh, and these pencil things that work like pens but without getting drippy or needing to be dipped or anything. Those are kind of cool.

And then she told us to sit down at the commonroom table in the inn and write down all our 'complaints' until we'd used them up and she didn't have to listen to them anymore.

And even more unfair?

She made Prince Daffyd do it, too, and *he* hadn't even been *saying* anything.

He didn't object then, either – though Amanita and I did. He just looked resigned and started doing it.

And Puck just smirked at us from across the room.

I was going to refuse – I mean, can't we even have a *conversation?* But then Amanita caved, and I got a look at that Commander Zaja. I never thought a *woman* could look that scary.

Well, I guess she's not as scary as Captain Shalladra Stillheart. Or Lady Embersoul. Or the Dark-elf princess. But pretty scary, nonetheless.

And with my luck, she's going to read all this after we hand in our 'homework' and then make me write *more.*

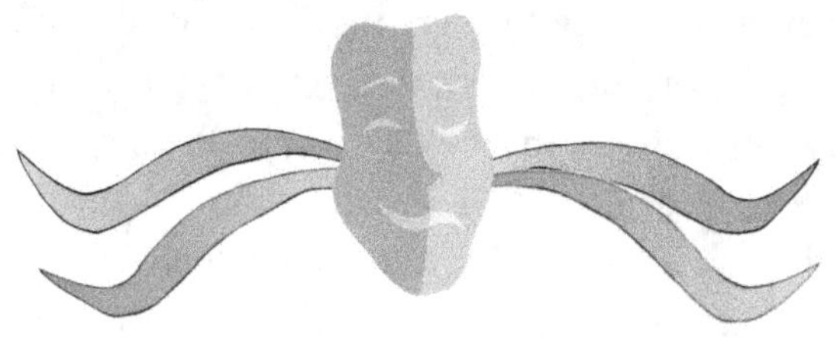

Day 18

of our Journey from Flowerdust to Pathremir

(They tell me it's the twenty-fourth day of the third month of Spring, but they seem to keep track of time differently here and I haven't gotten my hands on a calendar yet, so who knows what that means. Except that it's Spring.)

Well. Apparently, we 'get to' keep these little books. Commander Zaja rolled her eyes when I tried to give mine back last night and said something like "And you think I want to *read* more of what you're babbling about all *day?*"

And then she added an "Um, Your Highness," after Amanita and Puck both gave her the stink-eye.

I don't think she believes I'm really a prince.

And certainly not *Crown* Prince of Aldyrwald.

Nor does she really care.

Mostly that seems to have to do with me being a boy. She – and the other Guardswomen – treat Amanita with a great deal more deference, even if the results are the same. I'd say it was because she's *theirs,* but Daffyd gets treated more like me.

Right after we set down our pencils, Commander Zaja sent us up to bed.

Like we were *six.*

And Puck gets exempted from all of this... because, well, I guess because he's himself. 'Prince Skiftglow' as they're calling him now. He said we can keep calling him 'Puck' if we want, even if it's not strictly accurate anymore.

I don't understand any of this.

I'm not even sure why I'm writing this stuff down...

Well, except for the fact that I get locked up in a room with Prince Daffyd just after sunset every night. With guards on the door – more of those scary-looking short women. I think Amanita gets locked into her own room with her own guards.

And I don't know *what* they do with Puck, but there is absolutely nothing to do in *our* room.

You'd think that Twinklestar would object to this treatment of his unicorn-maiden, but noooo.

He seems to think he's done me sufficient favors by staying in his big size form and consenting to wear a saddle *(that Puck had made specifically for him by the best saddler in Flowerdust)* and a hackamore, so I have reins to hold on with.

And apparently, he's casting some kind of illusion so that he doesn't look like a unicorn while we travel. Which you'd *think* would mean I wouldn't have to wear the stupid white *robe.* But Puck pointed out that the Pathremiri women treat me a little better when I have the stupid thing on, so I'm stuck with that.

And Twinklestar spends the whole day trying to make nice to Puck's fairy-horse, Chillabiaen. Which means he is totally ignoring how he's jouncing me around in the saddle. You can't post for a trot when your stupid steed decides to randomly break into a canter or slow to a walk. Or do some dancing steps or...

Chillabiaen is ignoring him as much as possible, for which I don't blame her. Twinklestar acted like he'd forgotten she existed when Rainsparkle showed up. Not that Chillabiaen had been around at the time, but it was still pretty sleazy behavior in my book. And in Chilli's apparently.

Puck – who is stuck riding next to me while all of this is going on, thinks it's all terribly funny.

Well, he does until Chilli gives him a *look* over her shoulder and then they move up next to the commander. I'm not sure who I feel most sorry for at those moments. Puck, for having to talk to Commander Zaja, or Twinklestar, who always looks so dejected, for all that he *totally deserves it.*

Or me, who has to listen to my unicorn mooning on about his love-life for hours after that.

GODS, this 'falling in love' stuff is stupid.

At least at that point, Amanita usually comes over to ride with me. She's usually done fighting with her brother for awhile by then.

That gets kind of noisy, honestly.

Especially when it devolves into the two of them singing out obscure insults. 'Daffy Daffyd daffodil' at least seems a play off of his name, but why *he* calls *her* 'poisonous mushroom' I have no earthly idea.

I can sort of see Commander Zaja's point actually. Or I could, if she weren't set on punishing someone along with Amanita – who is the one who always starts it.

Daffyd's not a bad sort... he doesn't leave dirty socks lying around or drink out of the water pitcher or anything. Or snore. But he's over there on the other bed scratching away in his own book, so I suppose he doesn't really want to talk.

And, oh, my GOD, but this is way too boring for all the work it took to run away from home... start on my Bold Quest and become a Hero.

They called us that in *Flowerdust* anyways...

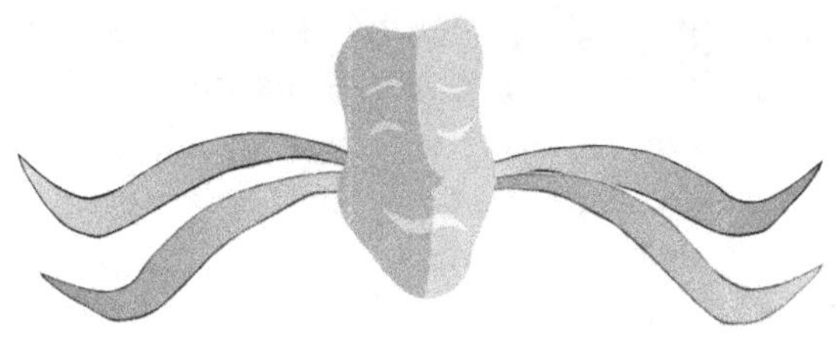

Day 19

of the Journey

Well... this might be getting a little more interesting.

While we were riding today, Daffyd explained that we can't talk much after they send us to bed because the Guards will report us. The doors and walls of these inns are pretty thin, and those girl-fighters are apparently as nosy and gossipy as Mama's ladies-in-waiting back home. Girls are girls everywhere, I guess.

He says this 'journaling' business is the only way he managed to stay sane before he found us.

I don't know many details yet, but it sounds like leaving Pathremir to hunt for his little sister was *his* idea and he got saddled with this pack of nanny-guards because he did it the *proper* way and went through 'channels.' Meaning he got his grandmother-the-Queen's approval.

I *knew* sneaking out was the right approach.

Papa might have agreed with me – I mean, *he* went on *his* Quest to win Mama and he didn't take a whole troop with *him*. It's just the way things are done in the Mountain-Region. But Mama would have insisted.

And, to be fair, I suppose I could see why. Aldyrwald wasn't under threat of invasion if something happened to Papa when *he* was Crown Prince. He has six younger brothers, after all, even if Uncle Louis is the only one who would probably have been acceptable as an alternate Heir, since he's the youngest.

Anyways, things might be getting more interesting because there is currently a big fight – er, *debate* – going on in the room next door between Amanita and Commander Zaja and Puck.

Daffyd has his ear to the wall, but I figure I'll get the details tomorrow and none of the names of people and places really mean anything to me anyways. I'm tired of listening to Amanita yelling about stuff for now.

We've apparently crossed over a border (*another* border... the countries on these 'Central Plains' are just as small and snarly as the ones at home) into a bigger and more stable country called 'Dysacha.'

Oh, there's Daffyd, and he's smirking. Something interesting must have been decided.

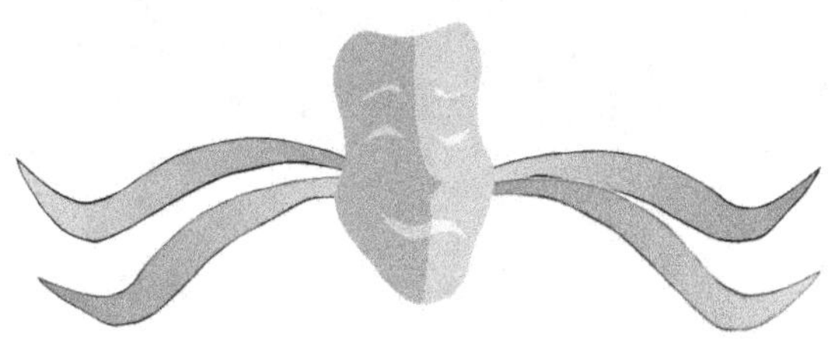

Day 20

of our journey

So, today Amanita was in a total grump and everyone tried to avoid her while we rode along what someone has *finally* explained is called the 'Tea Road.' Apparently, that's the name because the best tea is grown in that Darjil place where Valderon Raven'sWing enchanted the whole populace, and then it's transported up here for sale around the world.

Getting hold of a *map* has been nearly as hard as getting hold of a *calendar.*

And, honestly, I could probably just ask, and someone would show me one or explain, or something. But there hasn't been much of an opportunity to ask anyone. Commander Zaja likes it quiet at meals, and nobody goes against her. And I really want to see this stuff written down, so asking while we're riding is probably not a good idea; I haven't *tried* reading while riding yet, but my stomach gets tickly in a bad way, just thinking about it.

Though Puck does it all the time, since Chillabiaen doesn't need direction any more than Twinklestar does.

Hunh. Which means if I could get over my guts, I could probably do it.

Anyways, I'm going to try talking to Daffyd in a few minutes. If we whisper, maybe I can get some more details of what's going on out of him. *He* seems to know what's going on, but when he tried to explain last night, we got the guards pounding on the door and telling us to 'quiet down.'

Nanny-goats, all of them.

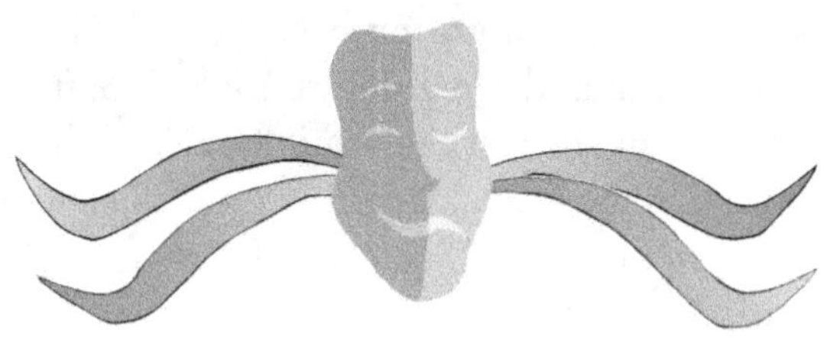

Day 21

of our journey

Well, we've left the Tea Road.

Daffyd was finally willing to explain – in whispers – last night.

He is *super cool,* by the way. He's about a year older than I am and in kind of the same boat, except he won't ever be King of Pathremir. So, all he gets is to be marriage-bait... and he went on this mission to look for Amanita partly to get away from all that.

Their mom and dad are arguing that neither of their kids should have to get married until they're at least twenty – fully adult here, though it's twenty-one for me at home – and he says his Grandmother-the-Queen agrees. But their other grandmother – their father's mother, the one Amanita doesn't like – is pushing for sooner. A lot sooner.

Like, *now.*

Daffyd is sixteen, so he *could* legally get married. And Amanita's too young, but she could be betrothed. That's more or less the way it is at home, too.

He seems more concerned about his own situation than hers. I gather there aren't a great many spectacular options for Amanita, but he's not as important in their scheme of things, so they can just pick someone and do the deed.

There's some complicated junk about the way they're all related and how the succession works in Pathremir that didn't make sense to me but apparently explains the unpleasant grandmother's reasoning. I'll try to figure that out another time.

Anyways, Amanita's in a grump because we're heading up to the capitol city of Dysacha and are going to make a State Visit out of it. She didn't want to, but she lost the argument. And she seems to think that Commander Zaja and Puck shouldn't have been able to overrule her. Because of her being the Princess of Pathremir and all – even though she's still just a kid.

Daffyd's smirk, night before last, was because *he* didn't think they'd manage to do it either.

He cares about Amanita, but he says she's been a little too full of her own importance ever since she was a baby. Everyone has been treating her like the best thing since a warm breeze in late Winter because of some more stuff that didn't make sense about their royal succession, but essentially there was no Heir at all until she was born despite their mom being the queen's only daughter.

"How *Môthir* didn't end up like Amanita, I don't know," Daffyd said. "*Môthir* is so self-effacing I think half the household staff forgets she's the Princess-Heir most of the time." And he'd sighed. "Maybe if she – and *Vathir* – were a bit more assertive it would have helped. Maybe they could have stopped everyone *else* from treating Amanita like the Second Coming of Varella the Wise."

Interesting...

And it was probably a good thing that we have only these dim little lamps in our room. I'm guessing my face was probably pretty red.

Because, well, the ruling of Aldyrwald was going to be going to another family than the Devinthals if *I* hadn't been born. Joanna would have had to do the usual 'languishing princess' deal and her husband would have been Papa's Heir and their kids would have carried *his* name. *(And it couldn't have been Roger, no matter how much he and Jo loved each other, because he's only a middleborn prince.)*

And then, of course, Prissy was born when Joanna was nine. And Prissy's tail messed *everything* up.

I, um, kind of *was* treated like Aldyrwald's savior.

Though I don't think anyone compared me to any of our old hero-kings. At least not since the incident with the frogs at Joanna's sixteenth birthday party. I wasn't really paying much attention before that, but I definitely got the biggest slices of cake, and to sit on Papa's lap more and everything.

Of course, I *was* the youngest... and it wasn't like Prissy and Jo got treated *badly* or anything.

But without my sisters – and Roger, who was there all the time as a squire until I was about eight, and as much of the time as he could manage after that – I probably *would* have a pretty inflated ego.

To be honest, Amanita's pretty down-to-earth most of the time. And it really seems to be more of a girls-rule-thing than a princess-heir-thing.

Daffyd seemed pleased to hear that she was willing to get her hands dirty working in the stables. I imagine keeping her head of a size to fit on her shoulders was sort of *his* job... rather like it was Prissy and Jo and Roger's with mine.

Um.

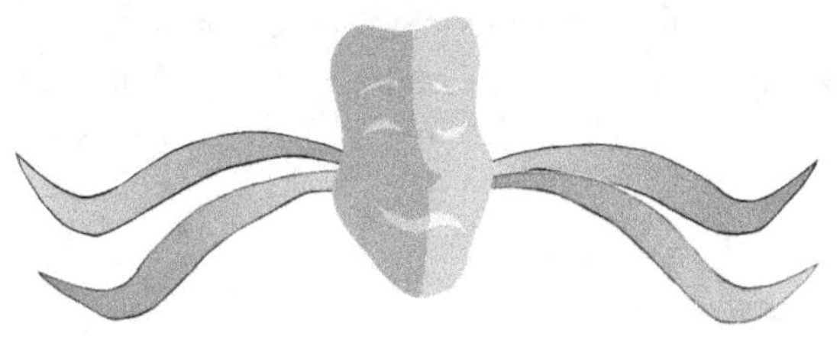

Day 22

of our journey

We have made it to Calabasha, the capitol of Dysacha.

Commander Zaja had us take rooms in what they *say* is an 'inn' – but it looks fancier than any castle in my storybooks. *Way* fancier than our castle at home.

And expensive, too, I gather, based on the way she winced as the servants showed us to our rooms.

There is filigree on *everything*. And I do mean *everything*. Like, on the seat in the washroom where you go you-know.

It's crazy.

And the windows are practically the *whole wall*. With a balcony, though the doors are locked, and given Commander Zaja's expression, they're staying that way.

And what I can see out there... whoa.

We're *six* stories up and higher than everything but the hill off to the right – the east? – that holds the royal palace. It seems like I'm looking out over as many roofs as there were blades of grass on those interminable Central Plains. I can't even see the streets from this angle, but my impression of the people as we rode in were that they look a lot like the people back home, even in the clothes they wear, but they're even darker-skinned than Amanita and her brother and the women guards.

They *sound* different, too, though I can't quite explain how. I've found myself sort of copying it, and the locals don't seem to notice, but Amanita and Daffyd have given me some weird looks. *They* sound kind of different, too, like they're speaking the way the locals are. But then why do they give *me* weird looks when *I* do it?

There's something shimmery and grey or dark blue out past the roofs. I'm wondering if it might be the *sea.* But I can't *(heh, heh)* actually *see* it very well, so hopefully I'll get a closer up look while we're here.

Daffyd and I are still sharing a room, technically. And, um, this time we're sharing a *bed.*

Which would be *weird,* if this bed wasn't big enough to sleep a family of eight without anyone feeling squished. He'll get his side and I'll get mine. Or one of us can go sleep on one of the couches in the sitting room, which is even larger than the bedroom.

There's a canopy over the bed and velvet drapes, just like at home. So, I guess it gets cold here at night in the Winter. It's pretty balmy right now, in my opinion. And – thank all the Gods, *not insanely hot,* like on the plains.

The commander said we're to wait here for a tailor to come and see to our clothes. She's sending word to the Court that we're here.

I told her I have a nice outfit in my saddlebags, and she gave me a disbelieving look and said to just wait. It's only just past noon, so I suppose there's time.

I hope they send up some food with the tailor.

Daffyd laughed and threw himself onto one of the couches once she was out of the room.

"Don't bother about unpacking, Thony," he said, waving a hand to stop me as I started to look for my good clothes. "We stayed in this place on the way down – which was one of the reasons we couldn't just slip through Dysacha the way my sister wanted to do. King Videl would be horribly offended. Royalty are supposed to do all the proper things when passing through. But the inn's servants will be annoyed if we see to our own things. And the tailor will want to freshen up our clothes anyways. There's probably some crazy new fashion at Court that we'll want him to set us up for."

He rolled his eyes. "Mine are still covered with these insane little bows from the last time. I looked like a holiday tree."

I frowned at him, but left my bags alone. The idea of someone sticking bows all over my one good suit of clothes is *not* appealing. "I can understand ironing them or whatever, but why do they need to alter our clothes? Shouldn't we look like we came from our own homelands? And... wouldn't yours *already* look right? How long ago did you come through, anyways?"

Daffyd shrugged. "Calabasha is the fashion capitol of the East. And we were here..." He pursed his lips. "About three months ago. So those little bows would probably make me a laughingstock by now, if it really works the way they explained it to me then."

I shook my head in bemusement. "That is *insane.* Hey, do you think they'll send us up some food?"

He winced. "Maybe if *you* ask. Zaja seems to think she can keep me from growing taller by not letting me eat."

He's already mentioned that Pathremiri women dislike tall men... and I've seen the disapproving looks he gets if he reaches for seconds at meals. And I'm sharing a room, so I can hear his stomach rumbling on the nights he doesn't.

"Do your parents actually approve of that?" I asked. "Or... your grandmother? The nice one?"

He shook his head. "No. At home I get to eat as much as I like – in private, anyways. It'd be hard to eat much at state banquets with all those women glowering at me... *Vathir* makes sure I get smaller than normal portions at dinner and then a proper meal before and after."

Pathremir... doesn't sound like where I really want to be going.

On the other hand, this world – and, to be honest, mine probably, too – seems a bit more dangerous than I really want to be wandering around in on my own.

Yet, anyways. I need to learn some more skill with my sword and bow. Puck has agreed to teach me, and Commander Zaja looked amused and disapproving at the same time, but she didn't forbid us.

She's just kept us moving too fast and then locked me up every night so there's been no chance.

But I've already managed to clarify that there are no princesses besides Amanita (and her mother) in Pathremir. So clearly, I *will* have to go *somewhere* else. Eventually.

I wish I could have gone south with Dae and her friends.

Well, I sort of wish. I've heard it's even hotter as you go farther south. And it's getting on towards Summer. Even Istevan didn't seem happy about that part of it. And Pathremir is in the mountains, I remember that much from Shalladra's map.

I am so *sick* of all this *flatness* and *grass.*

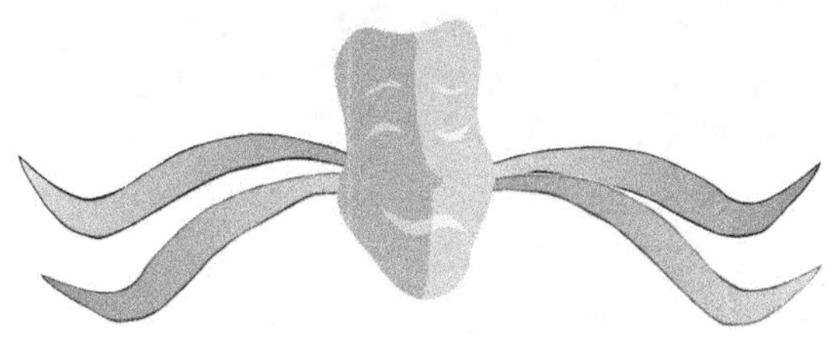

Day 30

of our journey

Zaja ordered us to journal again tonight. Is it *my* fault that Amanita is getting super-antsy as we approach Dysacha's border with Selavan?

Oh, wow.

I haven't done this in over a week.

Well.

Calabasha was... disappointing.

King Videl was old and fat. His daughter, the Crown Princess Evelynne was... old and fat. *Her* daughter is apparently a recluse and refuses to come to Court or bring her family in – she's supposedly beautiful, but she's also thirty, married, and a mother.

The courtiers are mostly old and fat.

And covered in silk flowers that are attached to everyone's clothes in places that seem... rather inappropriate, even though their apparel was otherwise quite modest. By Aldyrwald standards, anyways. Commander Zaja was appalled and let Amanita insist that we leave after only a couple of days. *Our* clothes were, um, 'de-flowered' by some of her junior warrior-women *(I absolutely refuse to call them 'Privates' in this context, even if that is the proper term for their rank)* before we even departed.

There was a rumor that the younger Dysachy nobles are gathering around the younger princess and she has an informal Court off in her country palace or whatever. And that the princess isn't so much a recluse as very disapproving of the debauchery of her grandfather's Court.

We didn't see any debauchery *(besides the weird placement of the flowers)*. But I'm not sure what that would look like exactly anyways, so maybe I just missed it.

No chance of finding my princess there, anyways.

Thank goodness, I guess.

Daffyd says that the glittery stuff out north of the city *was* the sea and that Zaja and Amanita should have let us all go see it. But they didn't.

Which is annoying. I've wanted to see what that much water looks like ever since Uncle Louis found his mermaid princess and started sending us those nasty barrels of pickled fish.

Daffyd says that we have to go through the whole royal rigamarole in Selavan, and that there is No Way we can miss seeing the sea there, since the king's castle is right on a cliff overlooking the sea.

I wonder if there are mermaids.

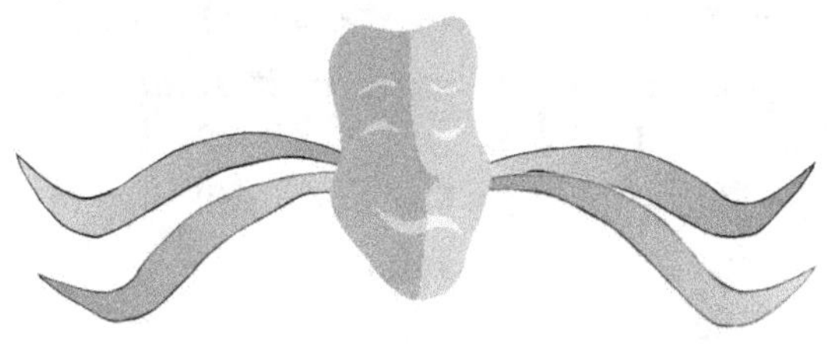

Day 35

of our journey

I finally mentioned to Daffyd that I haven't got a clue of where we are, and he looked surprised and pulled a leather map-tube out of his bags. He was so nice and offhanded about it that I felt like an idiot for not having brought this up before.

Of course I'd been exaggerating. I had *some* ideas, based on Shalladra's map. Which I *really* wish I'd kept, but I think it ended up with Davril and Istevan.

And once the Pathremiri prince spread out his map for me to look at, I decided to ask the question that I'd been wondering about, based on my vague memories of Shalladra's map.

And now I feel like a *total* idiot.

What I asked was why we were taking the very long way to Pathremir instead of cutting across the Plains of Gavenor. Which – *if I had been paying attention* – I would totally have known the answer to. But I was thinking about my lessons on triangles and we are essentially traveling the legs of a ginormous right triangle. By my guesstimate – I don't have the actual numbers yet, since he put the map away – but we're going something over fifty percent farther than cutting across the Plains.

Daffyd gave me this sideways look. "You're kidding, right? I mean, I know you're *not from around here–*" this has become our catchphrase for having crossed the Fairy Wood from another world, "–so maybe you don't know about the demons. But I'm sure you can see on the map that there's no roads or rivers. That place is almost as dry and featureless as the Muana, even if it's not nearly so large."

(The 'Muana' is the ginormous desert far to the south. Amanita claims that no one even knows how big it is. I am skeptical.)

"Um, *demons?*" I asked.

Daffyd nodded soberly. "There are still people – humans and others – who live out there... but not many. And they're barely scraping by. I heard they hired the entire graduating class from Sonoro's School of Soldiering a few years ago, hoping *someone* would be able to exorcise the demon. It... went badly."

I frowned. "What would mercenaries be able to... oh."

And *that* was when I remembered that Shalladra Stillheart had taunted Kamauri about what had happened in the Plains of Gavenor when they were fighting.

I mean, granted it was almost two months ago now. And I'd been a bit more focused on what was happening right *then*.

But still. We don't hear about *demons* in the Mountain-Region so much that it should have slipped my mind.

"I guess... Kamauri and Rainsparkle were there," I muttered. "She said something about holding off a demon there. Just before you guys arrived, I think."

Daffyd nodded. "And supposedly a couple of the young dragons flew over from Dawil and helped get the mercenaries out before they all died. But even they didn't try to *fight* the demon."

The idea of demons and dragons fighting each other sort of boggles my mind.

Also, the way Amanita and Daffyd and, well, pretty much everyone I meet here just assumes that dragons are always the good guys. It makes me wonder about what's going on at home, where they are *never* painted as good guys in the stories I've heard. Maybe we have a different kind of dragons?

The Pathremiri prince had given me a wry look at that point. "I sort of had a crush on Kamauri from the stories that filtered up to us after that. I mean she's a *real Hero*. If Daennor hadn't been there with her in Flowerdust... I might have proposed to her. Even Grandmother Eldest-Princess Reyalla couldn't have objected if I brought home a *bona fide* Hero to be my bride. Even if it messes up her political plans."

I blinked a few times.

Kamauri was kind of pretty, I guess, but a woman who wielded a sword – or a spear – well enough to challenge demons and dark-elves doesn't really seem like marriage-material to *me*. I mean, what would be left for the *guy* to do?

I kept my mouth shut on that – Pathremiri guys probably have different things they're looking for in a wife – but Daffyd must have noticed I was biting my tongue. He gave me what I can only call a *measuring* look.

"My other so-called 'choices,' Thony, are rapidly narrowing. Grandmother Eldest-Princess Reyalla still feels *she* should have had the throne. She's been trying to out-politic my Grandmother-the-Queen for thirty years, and she's just about cornered Her Majesty into agreeing to give me in marriage to the Commander-General of the Armies. Who is, by the way, *older than one of my grandmothers*. I'd be her third husband – part of the negotiations are hanging up on whether she's willing to set the other two aside as concubines and give me the position of primary husband, since she's quite fond of them and has several adult children who are objecting. But the chance to wed a Prince of the Blood – even if she's probably too old to bear me a child – is pretty tempting."

That... sounded almost worse than what would have awaited me – still awaited me – at home.

But Daffyd wasn't done. "Grandmother-the-Queen has been avoiding agreeing as much because of the power it will bring the Eldest-Princess for having arranged this as because... well, because *Môthir* is refusing to give consent."

He gave a... wintry smile. "I'd *like* to believe that both of them are doing it for my best interests, but I have to be practical. I'm an asset – a *gift* to be given to bind some powerful woman closer to the throne. If Grandmother Eldest-Princess Reyalla had managed to hide her involvement in the scheme more effectively, I'd likely be wedded already."

I'd swallowed hard. This was just *too* close to home.

"But you think you could get away with bringing home a Hero wife?"

"Could *have?*" Daffyd shrugged. "I'd've damn well *tried*. Commander Zaja is probably under orders to keep me from doing any such thing... but I haven't done anything to make her think I could slip away from her, so our guards are hopefully less on the alert for that than women sneaking in at night to, ah, *spoil the goods*."

He looked wry. "The Commander-General *is* her boss, after all. *And* her cousin."

That... actually brought up something I'd been trying to ignore.

I tried to be discreet. "Um, Daffyd... those guardswomen... they keep, um, trying to catch you alone..."

Which didn't work all that well, considering that they made me stick to him like glue. About all I could do was pretend I wasn't seeing anything, especially when he looked... flustered and embarrassed and... kind of miserable about the whole thing.

He winced and rolled his eyes. "Yeah... well, I suppose they have fantasies of having a prince fall in love with them."

"They aren't trying anything like that with *me*," I pointed out.

He'd shrugged. "You're a foreigner. And a unicorn-maiden."

I couldn't mistake the envy in his gaze.

Apparently that stupid *robe* was doing me some good after all. Mama's ladies had just started getting a look in their eyes like that the last year or so before I'd left – after I started to get taller – but *Mountain-Region* maidens would never be so forward as these Pathremiri girl-guards.

But none of that answered my question. Apparently, I had to be a bit more direct.

Yuck.

"What I was trying to say," I went on, and I knew I was turning as red as my hair, "is that if they're supposed to be protecting you from, um, anyone messing with your, um..."

"*Purity?*" Daffyd suggested dryly, also looking rather red. Which probably was a better look for him with that dark brown hair and skin and no freckles. Not that there was anyone here to compare and criticize. Thank the Gods.

"Yeah, that," I muttered, trying not to look at him. "If that's what they're supposed to be doing, then, um, why...? Wouldn't that just get them in trouble with Commander Zaja or... or this Commander-General person... or even your queen?"

He sighed. "You say you're a Crown Prince yourself, Thony. You can't be this naïve."

"They think you'd throw over your royal title if they can make youx fall in love with them," I interpreted.

He nodded and I frowned. "But then you *wouldn't* be a prince anymore. And if *that's* all they want..."

Daffyd looked wry again. "I doubt they're thinking that far ahead. I've been told I'm reasonably good-looking, I suppose, though one can't trust one's mother or grandmother on that. Or the toadies around the Court. *Amanita,*" he added wryly, "says I look like a stuffed toad. But I imagine I can't trust her either. To a common soldier, a prince's title makes him handsome."

"Well, they're not wrong," I pointed out, then felt my face growing hotter as he looked at me oddly. "I mean, aesthetically speaking and all. But if you lost your title, you couldn't support them or anything and you'd lose *that* shine..."

He shook his head. "Like I said, I doubt they're thinking beyond the chance to 'catch a prince.' And a Pathremiri man doesn't 'support' his wife. It's the other way around. And... our children would still carry royal lines, even if they weren't in the succession."

This is SO STUPID.

Surely, they can see that Daffyd is too responsible to throw it all over to marry some private in his grandmother's army. On the other hand, Mama's ladies-in-waiting started flirting with *me* and *I* wasn't going to throw it all over for 'love' either. Even if it weren't obvious that Papa was going to pick a bride for me from the time I was a baby.

I'm trying to think if I've ever known girls who *weren't* so silly.

None of Mama's ladies, certainly.

Nor most of the princesses from the other mountain kingdoms. Not that any of them had ever thrown themselves at *me*... but I'd seen them flirting with other princes or even grown knights.

And Joanna and Priscilla had been in an entirely different category. To me, of course, but with that whole mess with Prissy's tail... Not that I could imagine either of them doing that sort of thing even otherwise. Though as an oldest princess, Jo had been destined for a queenship *some*where, even if not of Aldyrwald. Prissy, though... without the tail and beautiful as she was, surely *some*one would have decided to categorize her as a youngest princess and not a middleborn...

Jo is so serious, but Prissy – *would* she have been silly if she had the chance?

Ugh.

I really should *not* be thinking about my sisters like this, but who else?

Evrien Quickfoot, Dae, Kamauri... hmmn, mercenaries may not make a good comparison.

Shalladra Stillheart, Princess Opalsinger, Lady Embersoul... okay, no dark-elves either.

Julanna Silversea, who fell in love with an Evil Wizard...

Amanita, whose taste for vengeance might be a *little* overdeveloped...

Do I even *know* any 'normal' girls?

Those two we met in the Fairy Wood? Midele and... what was the other one's name? Midele seemed normal. Except for being half-dryad. And she wasn't silly.

Some of Jost's crew? There had been a few girls who seemed pretty sensible.

Hey, why is Daffyd *still* giving me the hairy eyeball when he glances up from his own writing?

Oh, *GODS*.

Amanita and Dae are so gossipy. Did one of them tell him that Jost *liked* me? Or did *Jost* say something? We spent nearly a week in Flowerdust before heading north...

And anything I say now is just going to make this *more weird*.

I think I'll put the pillow *over* my head tonight. Maybe I'll smother myself in my sleep and none of it will be my problem anymore.

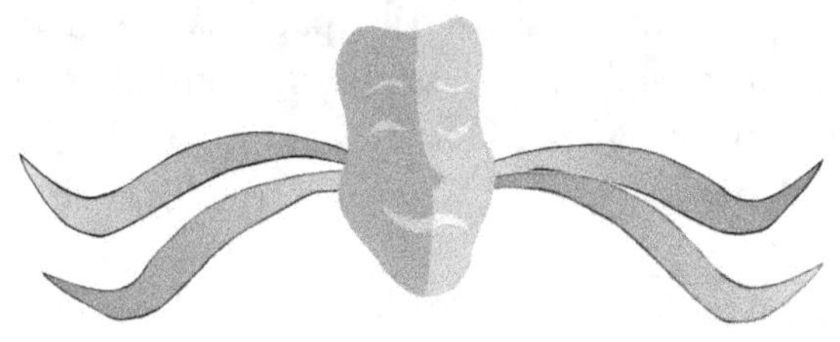

Day 42

of our journey from Flowerdust

Well, Daffyd's been a little weird with me for the past week, but we have no choice about sharing a room, so... it's wearing off.

Ugh. At least he didn't say anything to anyone else – or Amanita, at least, would be teasing me mercilessly by now.

Or have set him straight. One or the other. You can never tell with her.

We're in Dynsfyor, now. Which is the capitol city of Selavan... sort of.

The king and his Court are somewhere else – a couple hours ride away, I'm told. I imagine we'll see it, but we're waiting on an invitation and this one is more politically messy since Selavan and Pathremir aren't exactly on friendly terms.

Apparently, this is why we stopped in to see King Videl in Dysacha. It established that we're just making state visits to *everyone* along the way, nothing sneaky, nothing special. Davril had mentioned a few months ago that the two countries nearly fought a war when Amanita left, so this one is Very Important To Get Right.

Dysnfyor is HUGE. Like, even bigger than Calabasha. If not so gaudy.

*(And Daffyd and Amanita are giving me those **looks** again. If they think it's **rude** for me to try to talk like the locals, I wish they'd just say so straight out. I mean, the way the language keeps changing **feels** pretty weird in my mouth... but apparently I'm doing it well enough to communicate.)*

And we're staying with Davril's parents. We had messages for them and their business, the Keetering-and-Salwan Banking and Fiduciary Institution Private Limited, and we arrived in the city mid-morning, so Amanita insisted we stop and deliver the messages first thing.

And then Mr. Keetering *(Davril's father)* insisted we come to lunch.

And then Madame Keetering *(Davril's mother)* insisted we stay with them.

And, honestly, Keetering House is as well appointed as Aldyrwald Castle and much less 'tastelessly over-ornate' than the inn we'd used in Calabasha. *(That's a quote from one of Davril's sisters after we told them about our last major stop. Apparently, she's been to Calabasha. And stayed in the same inn.)*

Davril's sisters seem pretty not-silly. The oldest *(younger than him, so about eighteen)* is about to get married to some minor nobleman. The middle one is up at the university on the other side of Pathremir. *(Amanita decided to be condescending and explain to me what a **university** was – which I **knew already**, thank you very much. There's one in Uncle Louis' kingdom.)* The youngest one, Kyrista, is getting ready to go up to the university herself. And they're all bankers, like Davril.

So, I guess there *are* some not-silly girls.

A pity that their father doesn't have armies to lend me. Kyrista is no beauty, but I like her way of looking at things. She's younger than any of the middleborn princesses back home that I'd get saddled with. And she wouldn't be interested in trying to kill me.

Actually, she'd probably be bored out of her mind with our simple economy. I'm still trying to understand what *banking* is. Every time I get it to make sense, they add in some other facet and it all goes out the window again. Davril was teaching me stuff when we were in Flowerdust, and Kyrista seems determined to pick up where he left off.

On second thought, I don't want a wife who thinks she's smarter than me and has to keep teaching me stuff.

She'd make a good *friend*, though, if we stayed long enough. She's already managed to talk Commander Zaja into letting us all go down to the docks tomorrow to look at the ocean.

*(Amanita decided to explain docks, and I had to point out that we spent the whole first half of this trip traveling alongside the river that the Tea Road parallels. I've seen **docks** at every little town. And I made sure to wonder **loudly** about why we couldn't load all the horses and everyone onto one of the freight barges instead of riding the whole way, since everyone says boats are faster. No one has yet answered me when I've asked this. I think they're all embarrassed that the 'rube who's from another world' figured that one out and they didn't.)*

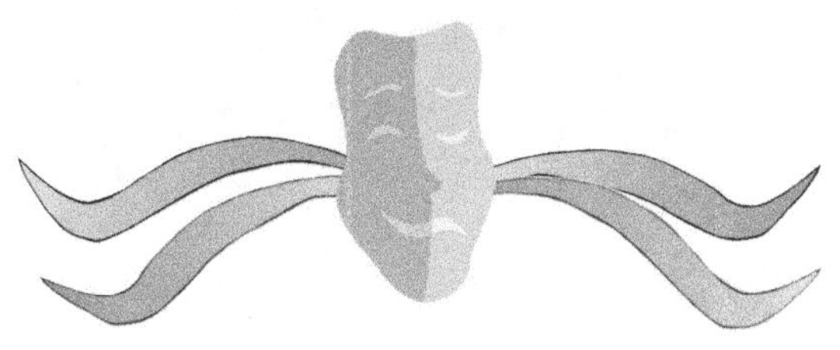

Day 43

of our journey

The sea – or ocean, or whatever they call it – is BEYOND WORDS.

I'm not sure if I think it's *amazing* or *terrifying*.

I just know I don't have any desire to go mermaid hunting anymore.

Uncle Louis must be way more of a badass than I ever imagined.

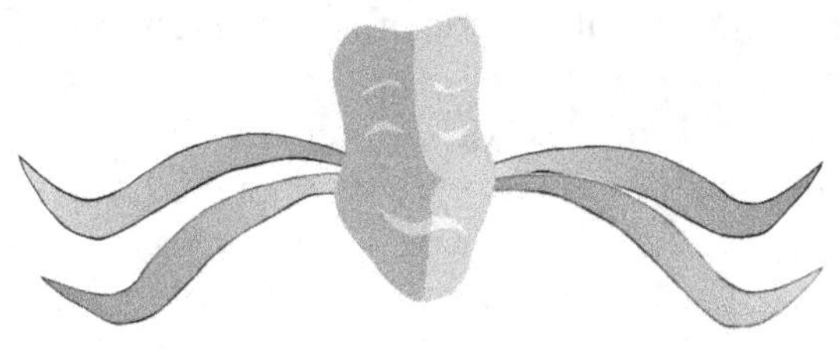

Day 44

of our journey

Still waiting to hear back from King Mithral's Court. Amanita wants to leave. Puck and Daffyd and Commander Zaja – and Davril's parents – are all against us leaving.

I'm tentatively on their side, but when Amanita flounced angrily into the Keetering House library and glared at me... I couldn't help but notice that her furious expression included eyes that were full of tears.

"I'll bet you're going to agree with everyone else," she said... and, well, she's my best friend, right? Except maybe for Twinklestar – not that my unicorn seems to think twice about *me* if there's a pretty filly around. He and Chillabiaen *(and the rest of our equines)* are, ah, *chilling* in a 'livery stable' nearby. I'm getting the occasional reports that the two of them are being treated like horsey royalty and having to listen to *(bad)* poetry about Chilli's eyes and... nostrils. (I don't pretend to understand how unicorns think.)

He's completely uninterested in *my* life.

Best bros – hah.

So, when Amanita said that, I shrugged as casually as I could. "I don't think I know enough to really have an opinion. It seems like asking for an invitation to Court and then leaving might be a bit... rude. But I know you well enough to believe you have reasons for wanting to go."

Good reasons might be something else entirely. But I had no doubt she has *reasons.*

The undersized Princess of Pathremir collapsed into an elegant wing-backed chair and gave me what might have been a grateful look. "Thanks. It's starting to feel like *everyone* is against me. It's like they think that I'm still the twelve-year-old who ran away from home. And I had reasons for *that,* too," she added a little defiantly.

That... was sort of the opening I'd been awaiting for like the last three or four months. At least.

"Yeah?" I said, trying to sound encouraging, but not so interested that she'd clam up again. Like all the *other* times I'd asked. I leaned as casually as I could against another wing-backed chair.

"Yeah." Amanita had shuffled her feet around, then looked up at me, those tears showing again, but not coming out. "*You* believe me, *don't* you, Thony? *You're* the Heir to *your* country. *You* know what kind of pressures I'm under. *You're* on my side, *aren't* you?"

"Sure," I said. "Though it would be easier to be on your side if I knew why we have sides. And maybe why you left home in the first place. You know why *I* did," I pointed out rather, er, *pointedly.*

The Selavani people are generally pretty tall – Davril's family is short by their standards, but even they are taller than what seems to be the average for a Pathermiri person. And Amanita seems to be small even for her own people, though that might be because she's not full-grown. And the chair she was in was built to Selavani standards. So she managed to twiddle a foot, since both her feet were dangling.

"I suppose..." She still sounded reluctant, so I sighed as theatrically as I could and threw myself into my own chair sideways, dangling both *my* legs over one arm. Amanita is always so super-touchy about being short; I wasn't sure if she'd take umbrage just because *my* feet touch the floor.

"I can't help if I don't know what's going on," I told her. "I can't even sympathize properly. Why *did* you leave home? Daffyd says they were trying to betroth you to someone," I added helpfully to get her started.

She snorted in a more Amanita-esque manner. "Not *me.* Not *yet,* anyways. But they *were* planning to do that to *him.* And... and there wasn't anything I could do to *stop* it. Except not be there. I figured as long as I was *alive,* but not *present,* that would be a reasonable argument not to get him hitched. I mean, have my only brother get married with me not even there? Not happening. *Vathir* agreed," she added, looking at me a little sideways.

"Hunh." I tried to stay as neutral as I could. That was... rather more selfless of her than I'd expected. It was also interesting that she'd confided in her father. I mean *I* had in *mine*... but Papa was the King of Aldyrwald and *her* father sounded like... some sort of minor functionary. Or not even that much. Didn't she say once that he *herded sheep* to escape being around his mother?

Amanita flushed a bit. "I mean, that wasn't the *only* reason. They never let me do anything at home. How am I supposed to learn to be a good and wise queen if I don't know anything about the world beyond Pathremir?"

"That makes sense," I agreed. "I kept telling Papa that I should get to at least visit *Schwannsberg.*" Or one of the other two valleys that made up Aldyrwald. Or the village on the other side of the mini-forest in our main valley. Or even just up on the mountainsides around the castle.

Or, you know, *something.*

I guess we really *were* on the same page. Though that didn't answer anything about our current predicament. But she was looking clammed up again.

"So... you left home to learn about the world and keep Daffyd from being married off too young," I summarized. Which protection would presumably end once we all got to Pathremir, but she'd bought her brother two years. *I'd've* appreciated that. "What about right *now?* What's up with *this* place?"

There was a long moment of silence.

I mean loooong.

If I hadn't been watching her while she fidgeted, I'd've guessed she'd fallen asleep.

If I hadn't learned the value of waiting someone out by now, I'd've said something, but Davril and Istevan and Jost had all used it really effectively. On me, among other people. Patience is not my favorite thing, but *waiting* seems like a useful skill to learn, so I'm trying.

This was the longest I've had to *wait,* though.

It was absolutely excruciating, and I *almost* gave up before she caved.

"I *hate* this place," Amanita burst out at last, and I wasn't sure whether I was more interested in what she was going to say, more relieved that the *waiting* thing was done, or more proud of myself for winning.

But then I saw the tears rolling down her cheeks.

It's not *winning* when your best friend is crying.

"I absolutely *hate* it," she went on. "I mean, Davril's family are nice people and all. But like he told us in Flowerdust, *his* people are the descendants of the ones that the *Líonar* conquered when *my* ancestress, Queen Varella, kicked them out of Pathremir, so I suppose I owe them something."

I remembered that conversation. Davril had said a lot more than that, though. He'd pointed out that both he *and* Amanita had mixed blood, because some of their ancestors had been these *Líonar* people. Amanita... had not taken that terribly well.

"So... just who are – or were – the *Líonar?*" I asked. "You say they came *here*, but Davril's family isn't... *Líonar.* So, what happened to them? Where did they go?"

I'd picked up some of the story, but not enough to really understand.

She waved a hand around in a hopeless, frustrated gesture. "They're all of them. The Selavani. Well, their nobility, anyways. They came down from the mountains and crushed Davril's ancestors two thousand years ago. Just like they'd crushed *mine* a thousand years before *that.*"

"Hmmn." I sat up a bit more properly and leaned my elbows on my knees to look interested. "Maybe you can start at the beginning?"

She fidgeted a bit.

"My people are the descendants of Mist-Maidens and Jewel Dragons," she said, then looked quickly at me. To see if I looked skeptical, I assume.

"I'm not going to ask how that worked," I commented as neutrally as I could, and got a wry grin back.

"I'm not sure either, actually. There might have been some shapechanging involved. And I think there were some humans in the mix as well. Short, dark people. Like me." She gestured at her own small body. "And our Goddess was the Silver Dragon of Gentle Darkness, the Lady of Forests and Wild Places. Her Name is Silvestria."

She sighed a little petulantly, and I frowned.

"You said that before," I remembered. "But I thought Puck's mom is the Queen of the Snow-Fairies and that She's your Goddess as well. How does She fit into this?"

Amanita looked away. "Queen Snowmistral. Also known as Sylphara of the Mountain-Breezes, Lady of Blizzards and Gales. I don't like to talk about Her. *She* chose the Líonar over *us*."

"But you like *Puck?*" I asked, trying to keep all of this sorted out in my head.

She shrugged, looking a little embarrassed. "He's... well, he's Puck. And... he pointed out that the Mist-Maidens are Snow-Fairies. So... we're kin."

At some distance, presumably.

"Okay," I said. "So, your country had this mix of human people and, um, dragon-people and... mist-people? Snow-people?"

She shrugged awkwardly. "They were all just... *people* people. At least the old stories mention that everyone got along and no one cared about ancestry."

Stories from three thousand years ago. And re-told with the purpose of uniting a bunch of survivors against the invaders who were now in charge. No chance *those* were 'adjusted' to make everything from before seem peachy.

Ha.

I'll just bet.

But right now, it's Amanita's perspective and the current situation that I need to understand.

"So, what happened?" I asked.

Amanita heaved another sigh. "On some *other* world, supposedly the *Líonar's* Gods decided They didn't need worshippers anymore and tried to fake Their Own deaths in some major battle. And the *trained* human seeresses all believed it. And the *Líonar* started to turn to a new God. Most of them actually *did,* as I understand it."

"Most, but not *all,*" I interpreted. "And all the *trained* seeresses. So, there were untrained ones who saw through it?"

She nodded. "Just one, as far as I know. But she got a bunch of her people to listen and they kept right on worshiping their Gods. Except that somehow *Bound* the Gods to them, so They couldn't go on to do... whatever it was They wanted to go do. And... their Gods' solution was to get rid of Their worshippers."

I know my eyes widened at that description. "And by '*get rid of,*' you mean..."

"Kill them," Amanita agreed. "So... they fled. The worshippers, I mean. I don't know why they didn't just ditch Karia – the young seeress – and follow the new God. Save themselves that way. But they decided to flee *and* keep worshiping the Gods they were fleeing *from*. Idiots."

"Idiots," I agreed faintly.

I could see it, though. *My* world had lost all of our Gods in something called a Ragnarök. Joanna and Priscilla and Roger said the Old Gods had all died, but there isn't really any *evidence* for that. My sisters' and brother-in-law's powers are undeniable, but they *could* just have become super-powerful wizards. It would be a lot easier of an explanation, honestly.

No one has been trying to spread the word of the Ragnarök beyond Aldyrwald, not even Joanna and her friends *(or Her Friends)*, though the word has filtered down to our own peasants and *they* clearly aren't sure *what* to think. Jo told Mama and Papa and me that everyone will come around in time and there's no real rush – I guess they were talking several generations, given how sad Joanna looked when she said it. After all, Gods can expect to live forever. Or almost forever.

Apparently, my world isn't to experience a penalty for still believing in the Old Gods, though. So maybe They really *have* all died.

"*Brave* idiots, though," Amanita said a little reluctantly. "I mean, they were actually defying the very Gods they believed in. There's all sorts of unbelievable legends about their flight..."

"Are you telling the story of the *Líonar's* Crossing of the Worlds?" Davril's sister Kyrista had wandered into the library without either of us noticing. "It's pretty exciting."

"Just a sketch of it," Amanita told her, and made a face. "I guess *exciting* is a fair word. The short version is that they were finally cornered in a canyon and the Guardian of the Ways Between the Worlds opened a passage to let them flee to this world."

"And then She sealed it behind them," Kyrista added, "and placed a great monster to guard the sealed passage so that the Old Gods couldn't come through after them."

Amanita glared at her. "It wasn't a '*monster.*' It was our *Goddess*, the Silver Dragon. And She *stayed* there for a thousand years while *our* people were subjugated and destroyed."

Kyrista Keetering looked entirely unruffled. "Clearly not *destroyed*. *You're* here now, after all."

Amanita's lips pursed. "If you were anyone else..."

And Kyrista actually *smirked*. Which seemed a little rude at that point, honestly, given how upset Amanita was.

"I'm not, though, am I? My ancestors went through the exact same thing. Arguably we're *still* going through it. We just made it work out a bit better. For the last *two* thousand years. Since Varella and her daughters kicked them out of Pathremir and *we* had to deal with them."

Amanita looked... like she'd bitten into one of those very sour fruits that Uncle Louis sends up from the coast along with the pickled fish. The pointy-ended yellow ones with the tough rinds. The cooks love them, and when you cut them crosswise they look a lot like the candied slices of the orange ones they get from the traveling merchants, but I tried one and – *UGH*. Bitter and sour at the *same time*. I saw David – one of Amanita's nemeses from the Aldyrwald castle kitchens – try one and his face looked about like hers did right then.

Come to think of it, Amanita had looked about like that when Davril had pointed out that she – *and* he, and therefore presumably his *sister* here also – had *Líonar* blood mixed into their heritage as well. My guess is that – at least on Amanita's side – it, ah, wasn't by her ancestor's choice, so I can see why she'd be touchy about it. Just because it's been five hundred years since the Mountain-Region forged a peace doesn't mean the old scars from the centuries of warfare aren't still there.

And honestly, Aldyrwald – and the Devinthal family – came out pretty well from that time. Which, in addition to current political realities, is probably *another* reason why our neighbors are less willing to 'forgive' Prissy for having a tail and let me marry a princess the normal way... and in the normal timeframe.

I'd say 'what comes around goes around'... but as Kyrista just pointed out, it's been two *thousand* years since Amanita's people kicked these *Líonar* types out. Which is a little long to hold a grudge.

I might be developing a certain sympathy for these *Líonar* folks.

"So... these, um, refugees from their own Gods ended up in Pathremir?" I asked, to try to get the story back on track. Amanita had never been so forthcoming before. I wanted as many details as I could get. "There must have been a lot of them, to take over like that. Didn't you say some of your people were, um, *dragons?*"

Not to mention having a *second Goddess* actively involved in all their lives that she *'didn't like to talk about.'*

The two girls looked at each other, apparently to see who was going to explain. Amanita looked... upset, and like she was trying to be mad and strong all at once. Kyrista looked... I don't know how you can look *serene with equanimity* at the same time as *slightly mischievous...* but she managed it.

After an awkward moment, Kyrista made an 'after you' sort of gesture. She's very graceful about these things. And she wears her very pretty gowns very well.

Amanita looked a bit like a horse in a dress when Commander Zaja made her wear one in Calabasha... well, until she was actually *at* Court. Then she'd glided around and curtsied and stuff like she'd been wearing floor-length gowns since she could walk.

I've seen a few of those Worthy Miller's Daughters who've become queens or princess-consorts, and you can always tell that *they didn't* grow up in floor-length gowns; their gracefulness is always a little too perfect and studied, like they're consciously aware of their skirts all the time.

So, I guess looking awkward is a choice Amanita makes because she doesn't want anyone to think she might be wearing a dress under anything but protest.

I suppose Pathremiri queens wear pants.

Weird.

Amanita gave the older girl a – well, it seemed more like a *token* glare, compared to the usual caliber she puts on those things – and turned back to me.

"Actually, it was just a handful. A few hundred people. But the Mist-folk at the time weren't warlike. The stories say they lived in small family groups here and there and only came together for festivals a few times a year. Even the dragon-kin... No one had ever done any *fighting.* Our Goddesses looked after us and there wasn't any *need...*"

"The *Lionar* are warriors," Kyrista chimed in, looking a little more sympathetic. "Then *and* now." She rolled her eyes. "Everything – and I do mean *everything* – has to be explained to them with warfare metaphors."

Amanita looked skeptical. "What happens if you don't? Do they just pretend they don't understand?"

Kyrista nodded. "Pretty much. That's mostly the nobility, though. We didn't have a lot of *them* for clients until my pretty cousin wrote that song and got His Most Effulgent Majesty to marry our Luminous Queen. Now the nobles all think Keetering-and-Salwan is hot stuff, and they all want accounts here."

She rolled her eyes again. "We've had to open up a whole new office at the castle, just to deal with them, since they don't want to come into the main bank like plebes. Or even have their trusted upper servants do it. And they want to see Papa *personally,* which kept him running back and forth to the castle several times a week until we could install Great-Uncle Edderhard up there permanently. *They* respect how white his whiskers are and it gets him *and* them out of everyone *else's* hair, so it all worked out."

She snickered. "They wanted Dav at first, until it was clear Istevan went with him. And the baby. So that meant *'and Julanna,'* since Daphne was still nursing."

Amanita looked confused. "King Mithral didn't want the most famous Bard in the world at his Court?"

But I finally had enough pieces of *something* to be able explain to *her.* "Julanna had just turned their whole world upside-down. I think the king and his Court might have felt like they'd seen enough of her for awhile."

Kyrista gave me what I'd like to think was an approving nod. "Exactly."

Which was all interesting, but I wanted the rest of the *story* that explained Amanita's extreme antipathy to these people. "So, a handful of refugee warriors came into Pathremir and took it over? From how many people?"

A few hundred didn't sound like 'a handful' to *me...* but they seemed to have larger numbers of people in this world. Or this part of this world. The Mountain-Region doesn't have *cities* like Dynsfyor or Calabasha *(or even Flowerdust, and now I could see why everyone else had called it a small town).* On the other hand, Uncle Louis' kingdom *does...*

I should write to him or visit or something when I get back. Even if I find my princess and don't need *his* armies as my backup plan anymore.

Amanita shrugged. "There's no way to guess at numbers. Small family groups, like I said. And... everything was really, well, *misty*. Like, really foggy. It's different now – I'm not sure why. At least the way the legends tell it, you couldn't see very far in any direction. We didn't call it *'Pathremir'* then," she added, sounding a little disconsolate. "It was the *'Land of Mists'.*"

Literally the 'mists of antiquity.' I wonder if all that *mist* was allegorical.

I probably shouldn't suggest that to Amanita, though. It takes away some of her explanation, and I don't think she'd take that very well.

"'Pathremir' translates as 'Reborn from Vengeance,' which is what Varella's people named it after they kicked the *Líonar* out," Kyrista explained. "The *Líonar* called it *'Loptheim'* in their language. Which translates to–"

"'Cloud Realm'," Amanita said, looking bitter again. "Pathremir is on a plateau. So, we're 'up in the clouds' compared to other places. The Cave where they Crossed from the other world is thousands of feet lower. I have no idea why they came all that way just to bother us."

"*Actually,*" Kyrista corrected her, "'*Loptheim*' can be better translated as *'Land of Mists'.*"

"You know their *language?*" Amanita looked torn between interest and disgust,

And she got a reproving look back. "It's *my* language, too. And *yours.*"

Because of that mixed ancestry, I assume. I'm not sure why Kyrista – and Davril back in Flowerdust – are pushing Amanita so hard on this point. It seems *really important* to them. Maybe because they want her to have a peaceful relationship with their homeland when she becomes queen someday?

To my surprise, Amanita looked more unnerved than upset this time.

She refocused on giving me more of this back-story. "Anyways, they conquered... us... one little group at a time. According to legend, they were greeted with open arms. Weary travelers and all that. And we had no tradition of fearing strangers. Supposedly they left a few people in each place, since no family-group could host such a number. And they arrived in the middle of Winter, so there wasn't as much food around to share. They left a few people behind at each homestead, before the rest moved on. And then, once they had people spread out in all these tiny isolated communities... they took over and enslaved everyone."

"Not exactly," Kyrista murmured, sitting down on a small sofa.

Amanita rolled her eyes. "Fine. They *enthralled* us. There's not much of a difference between a slave and a thrall."

Davril's sister shook her head. "Not what I meant. There was a gap of years – maybe even more than a few *decades* – between their arrival and when they took over. Karia's oldest son was involved, after all, and I think he wasn't even born until they came to Pathremir."

Amanita frowned.

"That's... interesting," I volunteered. "Why not do it immediately?"

Kyrista nodded at me. "A good question. Julanna did a lot of research into this at the university, before she wrote her song. Jess kept following it up, and Miki – that's our other sister, Mikeira, she's up there now – is still digging up stuff."

"What did they find out?" Amanita's tone could only have been described as reluctantly curious.

"Well, the *first* thing was that the *Lionar* were all exhausted when they made it to the Land of Mists. Sick, frostbitten, starving. All that stuff," Kyrista explained. "They lost something like half the number who Crossed the Worlds in the journey into the mountains. It took them a while to recuperate enough to contemplate anything besides surviving.

"And *then,* apparently there was a big difference of opinion amongst the *Lionar.* Karia – the young seeress that they'd followed into exile – wanted everyone to settle down – she was Chosen by the Goddess Sylphara once they got there, and still had visions to offer her people. But after all the tribulations they had gone through, most of the *Lionar* didn't want to follow her directives anymore."

"That... would be kind of fair," I had to comment. "I'd've been kind of upset with her myself."

Amanita glared at me. "Yeah, well, their *answer* was to go out and *enslave my people*. Who had been treating them like *honored guests.*"

"Not a cool reaction," I agreed, but I looked at Kyrista. "And kind of extreme. Any idea why they did that?"

"We're still working on that," Kyrista admitted, and–

*   *   *   *   *

Okay.

That was *way weird.*

I'm not even sure I want to try to write about that right now.

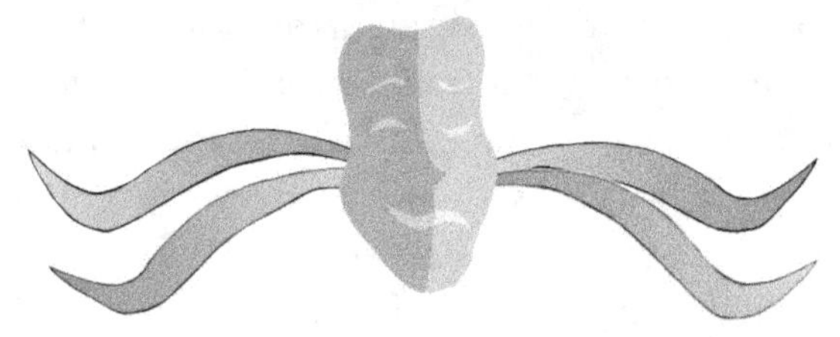

Later that night...

Okay, so I can't sleep.

I'm stewing about the crazy thing that happened.

Though, I suppose I'll be frustrated someday when I re-read this if I don't finish off that last bit, too. It's short, though. Kyrista didn't really have anything more to tell us, and Amanita was looking even grumpier, but it was time for dinner so we all put on our friendly faces. The food here in Keetering House is *amazing* and *way* better than anything I've eaten since I left home. And Davril and Kyrista's parents are awesome.

Kyrista *did* promise to take us somewhere tomorrow to talk to someone *else* who's looking into the whole why-the-*Líonar*-took-over thing.

So, I guess we'll maybe find out some more tomorrow? Though it sounds like this other person is a friend of hers, so I'm not sure why they would tell us things they haven't told Kyrista. Or maybe that's 'told her *yet.*' I guess that could make sense, if it's an ongoing project.

But what happened to make me stop writing was that someone was knocking on the door of my room. *(Did I mention how awesome it is that I've had a room to myself here in Keetering House? Well, it is. I had no idea that **privacy** would be what I would miss most about home. Well, privacy and Mama, I guess. Also weird, considering how much time I spent trying to stay out of her sight while I was there.)*

So, anyways, there was someone knocking.

So, I got up to check who it was – no biggie.

It was Daffyd.

Who, just to keep things straight here, has been a pretty cool guy during the month and a half I've gotten to know him. Not a prankster, but also not a tattle-tail. Good sense of humor. Not mean at all, no matter how snarky Amanita gets with him. Tends to try to soothe tempers *(mostly hers)*. A bit squished by all these overbearing women – including Amanita – but I guess I can see why. And did I mention that it was his idea to go out looking for her?

He's about a year older than me – a little taller, since I have *still* not gotten that growth spurt. *(Any day now... Papa and all my uncles – his six brothers and Mama's seven – are all reasonably tall people, so I know it **has** to be coming.)* He looks like Amanita – really dark hair that tends to turn a bit red in the sun, really dark eyes, and what I would have called 'really dark skin' before seeing some of the people on the streets here and in Calabasha.

And he's been kind of tight with Puck for most of this trip, since leaving Flowerdust.

Like, talking to him all the time, *watching* him all the time... even seeming to try to copy his *body language,* if that makes any sense.

I was wondering if he was crushing on Puck – but when I mentioned it, sort of jokingly, to Amanita she got... weird. Like, *really* weird. Offended, even.

What I gathered out of the lecture she spouted off was that she thinks – and, presumably this is a Pathremiri thing, but I suppose it could just be an Amanita-thing, or even a not-*my*-brother-thing... Anyways, she thinks it's *weird* for guys to like each other. Like the weird-to-the-point-of-*morally-wrong,* kind of weird. She seems to think that guys aren't responsible enough, or mature enough, or something, to be able to manage life without a woman around.

So, I'd asked her 'what about Davril and Istevan' – who seem to be managing just fine. They're pretty great dads to baby Daphne, too.

And she looked *super* uncomfortable, but then she brushed it off by noting that they have Julanna with them. And when I pointed out that they'd told us all that was temporary, and what did that have to do with anything anyways... Well, she got all huffy and said it isn't *proper* for a guy to go wandering around without a woman from his family to look after him and make sure that other women weren't leading him into temptation. Or something like that, anyways.

And Daffyd had come into the room we were in – this had been back in Calabasha when we were staying at that insanely fancy inn – and caught the end of that. And he'd rolled his eyes, but agreed that it's been a lot easier dealing with Commander Zaja and her troop since they found Amanita. I gather Commander Zaja is some kind of distant cousin of their mom or something, which is why she was made commander of his guards when he left Pathremir.

Anyways, I didn't write anything about that *then* because I didn't want to think about it. Amanita is a really good friend, and I kind of hate the idea that she'd be so close-minded as all that. And if I'd thought about it enough to write about it, I'd've had to wonder if *that* was why she followed me when I left Aldyrwald – I mean, I already *know* she thought I was a helpless little lamb in the Fairy Wood without her, but somehow this makes it even worse.

And... if we hadn't already been so far from Flowerdust and my other friends, I'd've been super-tempted to turn around and go back. Because, just *why* would I want to go to this country of hers that's so weird and condescending about guys?

Well, if we hadn't been so far *and* I didn't have Puck telling me that was what the Fairy Queen – the Goddess Who Is the Guardian of the Ways Between the Worlds – wants me to do before She'll allow me to go back home.

So... with all of that, I *totally* did not expect what happened last night.

Daffyd knocked, and I opened the door of my room.

And then he kind of pushed his way in, saying something about a pen I'd borrowed from him. Except I *hadn't* borrowed anything from him, so I was confused.

And as soon as he was inside, he pushed the door shut and latched it.

Then he turned around, took a step towards me and put his hands on my face and *kissed* me.

Which was... *so* not cool.

I mean. Dude should at least have *asked* first.

Jost had the manners to ask, and *he's* just a street-kid. Daffyd's a *prince*. He should *definitely* know better.

And then he stopped, looked at me, then did it *again.*

And then he stepped back, grinned at me like he'd done something awesome, and said "Don't look so surprised. You've been thinking about that for days now. You're pretty handsome, too."

And then he opened the door again and stepped out, saying something about "Fine, but I want it back when you find it," in an aggrieved tone as if it was the end of a conversation about that non-existent pen.

And then he shut the door.

And... oh my God, did I really just write 'and then he' like *five times in a row?*

I just stood there like an idiot.

The. Whole. Time.

I mean, I figured out that his nonsense about a pen was to throw off anyone who was out in the hallway. *(Madame Keetering forbade Commander Zaja from **officially** putting guards on our bedroom doors, and somehow managed to sort of convince her that Keetering House was safe for their princess... Yeah, their **princess,** like Daffyd – or I – don't even count. But I've seen some of those Pathremiri women sneaking around the place trying to look like they aren't sneaking around – they're really bad at it – and the Keeterings have a bunch of servants and family. So, I don't know who all might have been out there that Daffyd was speaking for.)*

And it's kind of dumb to be annoyed that some unknown person thinks I'm a total ditz who borrows other people's stuff and loses it.

But it's easier to be annoyed about that than figure out what the *heck* Daffyd was thinking.

Do I like, give off some kind of guy-attracting *scent* or something?

Because if that's it, I'm going to start bathing twice a day. Or more.

Not that I mind what Daffyd thinks. And it was sort of nice that he thinks I'm good-looking – I mean, Mama says that, but you can't really trust mothers about that kind of stuff. Not her ladies, either, given that they all seemed to have decided that the Devinthal Marital Issues *(meaning none of the neighbors wanting anything to do with us)* meant that *they* might have a chance at being Queen of Aldyrwald someday.

But this is just going to make things *weird* between us now.

And normally I'd talk to Amanita about weird stuff like this – I even told her and Dae about Jost, after all – but I can*not* tell her about this. I mean, her *brother?* With her weirdo ideas? She would totally freak. And then Commander Zaja would find out and...

...ugh. What a mess.

They'd probably lock Daffyd up to keep him safe from me or something. Or vice versa.

Hmmn.

On the up-side of that, I'd probably get my own room at the inns on the rest of our journey from here up to Pathremir. *(I assume I'll get my own space at their family's castle either way.)*

No... no.

Daffyd's a nice guy most of the time. I can't do that to him. At some point I get to leave Pathremir and this matriarchal nonsense behind, but *he'll* be stuck there.

I like him... just not like *that.*

Same as with Jost... though I think I could have liked *him* a little more like *that*... someday. Maybe. But Daffyd is just... too much like Amanita.

And... no.

Just... no.

.

.

.

But you know what's most bothering me?

*(And why the heck am I saying 'you'? This is **my** journal, and since I bought that magickal lockbox in Calabasha as a decoy, and a few extra blank books, and I've used that little spell Prissy taught me to make sure that the ones I've written in look blank inside if anyone opens them... **no one** is ever going to read this but **me**...)*

What's bothering me is that... that was *my* first kiss.

And... it wasn't *bad.* As I've noticed before, Daffyd has kissed most of the younger warriors in Zaja's troop. Or vice versa anyways. And he told me how that goes on with the younger noblewomen back in Pathremir as well. So, I imagine he's had lots of practice.

But a first kiss is supposed to be *magickal.*

It's supposed to be *amazing,* and make you believe you'd be ready to *die* for the person you kissed.

Papa said that's how it was for him and Mama. And *Roger* said it wasn't just hype, or parents telling parent-stories, it *was* really like that when he finally got to kiss Jo. And, well, Jeremy snickered a *lot*, but he eventually agreed, too.

And I... didn't really feel *anything*.

I mean, I felt his hands on my cheeks and his lips on mine. Even his eyelashes on my nose.

But it didn't *mean* anything.

And it's supposed to... isn't it?

It was a *first kiss*.

.

.

.

I... guess I should be *grateful* there weren't any... *sparks* or *magick* or *declarations of undying love* or anything.

I'm supposed to bring a *princess* home to Aldyrwald. One whose *father* has *armies* or *knights* to lend me. Not a prince, whose family might have the requisite warriors, but who'd be disinherited for breaking their traditions and mores, so he certainly wouldn't have access to those fighters to bring them to Aldyrwald.

And whose sister is my best friend.

And since *she's* the one with the armies at her beck and call...

Oh. That could get even messier.

Not that it *would,* because I *felt nothing at all.*

*(But, oh Gods, but can't you just imagine a whole pack of these tiny Pathremiri women facing down a troop of some of our neighbors' mounted knights? The neighbors would just laugh themselves off their horses. Of course, then they'd be on the ground and at a disadvantage when they found out how fierce these women are... Might be worth it... no. NO. I am **not** bringing home Amanita OR her whack-o brother.)*

(But maybe she has a cousin who would still have a claim on the royal armies? Even if she's not officially a princess?)

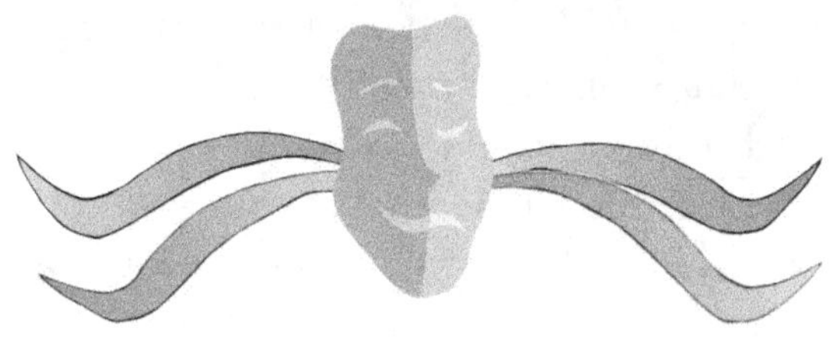

Day 45

Today was... not what I expected after yesterday. Though honestly? I'm not sure what I *did* expect.

Kyrista collected me and Amanita to go to meet this friend of hers.

The place we went looked like some ratty little shop entrance – we actually had to go *down* some stairs from street-level to get to the door.

And then once we were inside, we had to go up some stairs to get into the shop. And step over a row of sand-bags, so it appeared right away that flooding was a concern.

Which I could see as soon as we got past the stairs and sand-bags and I could look around.

I didn't know that many books existed in the worl– no, in the *universe*.

Wow.

The place is apparently called *Dauntless*, and it's a bookstore *(a **whole store** devoted to **books!**)* that is owned by one of King Mithral's top advisors, a sorceress widely known as Lady Wisdom. I gather that the purpose of the bookstore is more to have a name for what the place is and that she mostly acquires books, rather than selling them.

The place is actually run by Lady Wisdom's granddaughter, Inga. Insofar as sitting behind a desk reading whatever she likes all day counts as 'running' the place. If a book were actually purchased, presumably Inga would take the payment.

She is one of these *Líonar*-types that Amanita rails on about: golden-haired, fair-skinned, bright blue eyes... rather like Prissy actually, though Prissy's eyes are more green. She didn't seem quite as tall as the average *Líonar,* but that might have been my impression because she was hunched over her reading or reluctantly conversing with us while trying to get back to her reading.

Oh, and she wears glasses.

As Kyrista introduced us – which was sort of funny, since Amanita clearly didn't want to meet a *Líonar,* and Inga clearly didn't want to be dragged away from her reading – and explained about the bookstore, I got the impression that it was Inga's grandmother, Lady Wisdom, who we were coming to meet. When Amanita and I were turned loose to go look at all the books, I was pretty sure of it.

I think I wandered around for over an hour, mostly stunned.

It was like one of the caves that are in the mountains around Aldyrwald – and that I *finally* got to see because of Joanna's mountain growing into and taking over the back part of the castle when she suddenly became our Goddess of Earth. One of the old secret passageways now opens into one of those cave-tunnel-complex things that Jo says were made over the eons by dripping water – except the *mountain* wasn't there two years ago, so... I'm not really sure what she's talking about. Or what She's talking about, I suppose.

Anyways, the caves have these piles and teeth of stone reaching up from the floor and down from the ceiling and meeting in randomly placed pillars. And all the stone is glisteny with wet and with crystals 'growing' *(Jo's word)* on the walls. And all of it makes this mess of tunnels and passageways that you have to duck under and around and through, but it is totally worth it.

The Dauntless 'bookstore' was like that.

Except instead of wet, glisteny rock, there were *books.*

Rooms and *rooms* and *floors* of *books.*

(Sorry, Jo, this was WAY better.)

Just the idea that this many books could even exist...

Anyways, eventually I heard Kyrista calling my name and Amanita's, so I wandered back up to the entrance. Amanita got back around the same time and had *almost* as stunned an expression as mine must have been. Which made me feel a *little* better.

Inga gave us raised eyebrows and commented to Kyrista that she had better not take us to the public library. And Kyrista replied that Dauntless is much more interesting anyways.

And then they had to explain a 'public' library to me and I practically fell over in shock.

A place where *anyone* can just go in and read books? *Anyone?* For *free?*

At home, most of the commoners don't even know their letters.

I want to go see this place rather desperately now.

My reactions gave Amanita a chance to feel superior again. Apparently, she knew about the public library, though not about Dauntless. I'd've been annoyed if I wasn't so amazed... and if it didn't rub some of that raw, angry edge off of my friend's attitude. She was almost cordial with Inga after that.

And what Inga had to tell us – added on to what Kyrista already told us – was interesting.

Really interesting, but I could see it upset Amanita. Kyrista could tell as well, given how she kept wincing when she looked at Amanita.

I'm not sure if *Inga* could tell... but my guess is she's the type of person who's more interested in facts than people; not so much uncaring as entirely oblivious. But you can trust that sort not to hold stuff back that you *should* know, just because they know you'll find it unpleasant. I had a tutor like that for Geography when I was about ten, and I learned a ton, but he got dismissed after Mama got upset with things he said a few too many times.

Anyways, it was a lot of details about the early politics of the *Líonar* people after their Crossing of Worlds. Apparently, they broke up into factions after they recovered from that first, hard Winter – though most of this was written down a very long time later, transcribed from their oral tradition.

All that reverence for Bards that Amanita kept bringing up in Flowerdust. And that Davril agreed with.

Personally, I'm seeing more *similarities* between Selavani, Pathremiri, and *Líonar* culture than the other way around. Not that I'd mention this to Amanita, of course. Watching her head *actually* explode might be *interesting,* but it would be messy and I'd lose my best friend in the process.

Even this extreme 'matriarchy' business in Pathremir. The *Líonar* all followed that young seeress of theirs and then – according to Kyrista and Inga – a couple of the factions that broke off early on in their occupation of Pathremir had to do with the seeresses.

Yeah, more than one. Even the seeresses didn't agree with each other, I guess. One group ended up moving into the mountains on the other side of the Pathremiri plateau, and the other group ended up in the mountains on this side.

I'm unclear on when all these different things happened in relation to each other or to when the first Pathremiri queen, Varella, led the uprising that kicked the *Líonar* out. Inga did say that the bulk of the *Líonar* population fled this way – and it was a lot bigger number of people, given that it had been a thousand years since their Crossing of Worlds – but their deposed king and his sons went the other way and stayed closer to the plateau.

Kyrista says that the legends they've unearthed from some place called 'Mountainmeadow' claim that the king had to be dragged away to save his life, because he wouldn't voluntarily leave his wife and daughters. And that his oldest son died defending his father and younger brother and their close retainers from pursuit.

And... supposedly the king then pined away until he died.

Which sounds pretty tragic.

Amanita pointed out that the 'Lord of Mountainmeadow' is still called the 'King of the Mountains' by his followers nowadays... even though they've been vassals of some other country for a thousand years. So... she was a little skeptical of the 'pining away' story.

She also wasn't particularly thrilled to have it pointed out that the Lord of Mountainmeadow is of Mistlander descent, since Queen Varella was the mother of that line as much as of her own.

Inga didn't seem concerned.

She went on to explain that the Selavani Royal House was founded by a cadet branch of the original royal family – one that doesn't seem to have intermarried as much with the Mistlanders.

"And they kept it that way after they settled here in Selavan," Inga finished. "The royal family is as pure *Líonar* as they come. Which isn't, really, given the thousand years in Pathremir where there simply weren't enough people to keep a 'pure' lineage. But most of the other families intermarried with the indigenous people a bit more, so the royal line has some local bloodlines as well."

She rolled her eyes. "There's been a movement the last couple of generations to keep the *Líonar* bloodlines 'pure.' Which is ridiculous, even if it weren't impossible given the mixing that's already gone on. And since the *Líonar* mag– hmmm..."

We'd finally reached a line that even the oblivious Inga wasn't sure she should cross, but Kyrista shook her head and told her to go on.

Inga raised her eyebrows, but shrugged as if it really didn't matter to her.

"The native *Líonar* magicks are getting weaker. Grandmama and I think it's because of inbreeding – which has been worst for the royal family, of course. And that's a big problem because the Lord of Light Himself selects our next Effulgent King from among the available male candidates of the royal house – and it appears, from our research, that a certain natural gift for magick is part of the God's selection criteria."

She shook her head. "The most magickally talented members of the *Líonar* community were the seeresses – who have formed their own societies up in the mountain peaks above the plateau – and then the original royal family, half of whom migrated to Mountainmeadow, and the other half stayed in Pathremir."

"It's why we're relieved to have our new Luminous Queen," Kyrista commented at this point, while Amanita spluttered a bit at the description of her revered ancestresses as being 'half of the *Líonar* royal family of ancient Pathremir,' "especially those of us who understand about the inbreeding in the royal family. She's from the nearer group of seeresses," she explained as both Amanita and I must have looked confused. "Since they've been taking Pathremiri men as husbands all along, she's bringing in completely new bloodlines."

"And setting the fashion for it to be acceptable *not* to marry for 'purity' of *Líonar* heritage," Inga said, giving Kyrista wry look. "Which is handy for Jess, even if it's been useless for me..."

Kyrista gave her friend a sympathetic look and suggested we should head back to Keetering House. We never saw this 'Lady Wisdom' person at all, though Inga mentioned something about her grandmother being upstairs. I gather this history project is more of a deal between Inga and the Keetering siblings and her grandmother is only tangentially involved.

After we collected Commander Zaja and her troop *(who had hung out on the street while we browsed the bookstore after being told that no, they could not come in and if Selavan's greatest sorceress couldn't keep Amanita safe, it wouldn't do them any good to be in there with her anyhow)*, Kyrista explained what Inga had meant. That Kyrista's sister, Jessina, is marrying a *Líonar* nobleman we had known *(and Amanita'd had some rather unfriendly comments about that – privately, anyways)*.

But Inga is herself the youngest of a large and prominent family and there is pressure for her to 'marry well.' Her grandmother disagrees, and has taken Inga on as an unofficial apprentice... but her parents are still pushing for a marriage. And with Inga's rather intense disinterest in humans, as well as her glasses *(which are apparently seen as a sign of 'weakness' by these **Líonar**-types)*, she's not exactly turning the guys away in hordes.

A pity *she's* not a princess. Though I suppose I'd have to protect the Aldyrwald treasury from her book-buying sprees...

A *public library* and *all the commoners learning to read...*

I think I could live with what she did to my treasury.

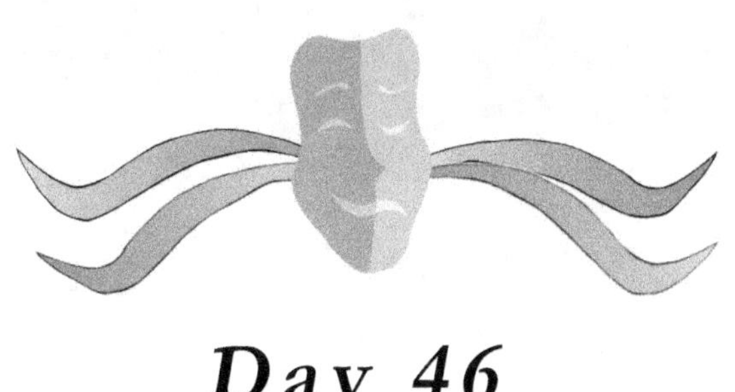

Day 46

Word has *finally* come that we are to go up to Court.

I am staying out of the way as much as possible while everyone else goes into a tizzy of preparation. And packing, since I gather we'll be staying up there.

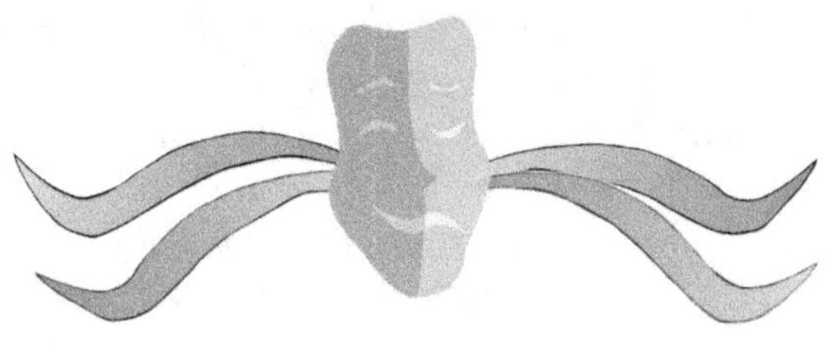

Day 47

It turned out that Inga decided to accompany us up to Court. Daffyd and Puck had been very curious about her after what Amanita and I told them, and they more or less monopolized her on the ride up.

Amanita and I got stuck listening to the younger guardswomen comparing notes on all the *tall Selavani men* who had been *curious* about them while they awaited us outside of Dauntless, day before yesterday. I'm coming to the conclusion that the supposed Pathremiri female preference for shorter *(and non-**Líonar**)* men is... not quite all it's cracked up to be. The discussions were... rather uncomfortable to have to listen to.

Commander Zaja ignored us all.

We stopped at a wayhouse a half-hour out from the castle to change into all those fancier clothes.

At least the long delay in getting our invitation gave us ample time to get outfitted properly. I did not bring anywhere *near* enough fancy clothes for these sorts of things, and Amanita had absolutely zilch with her before our visit to Calabasha. I like the way they do tunics here better than at home – it's more of a jacket-deal over the usual full-sleeved shirt; much handier for putting the fancy ones on and off without help. Amanita's dresses seem to have elaborate lacing in the back, so she's not as happy about the changes.

*(And thank the Gods – or rather Davril and Kyrista's family – for taking care of all that for me. I had more the idea that I'd be riding around in wilderness areas for some reason and did not bring anywhere near enough money. They've also changed mine out for local coins... a couple of times now, since Davril first got me set up in Flowerdust. I thought gold and silver were gold and silver no matter whose face was on them... but apparently there are differences in the purity of coin from different places, so they **aren't** all treated the same.)*

So then, all gussied up, we proceeded to ride into... what looked a great deal like the setup at home.

Not *exactly*, of course. Our castle is at the bottom of a valley *(and half eaten up by Joanna's Sacred Mountain now)*, and King Mithral's is at the top of a cliff overlooking the ocean. But the village at the foot of the castle looks about the same.

And... I have to say this with a certain amount of shame, now that I've seen how people live elsewhere... it looks pretty shabby.

"Well, *they* think a lot of themselves, don't they?" Amanita commented as we rode through the village. "I mean the setup is a lot like Aldyrwald, but it's like they took the basic concept and went for *intimidating castle and downtrodden people,* whereas you guys went for *'we're here for you, and let's all work together.'*"

That made me feel a lot better, even if I know it's mostly about how Amanita has Issues with the Selavani nobility.

It helped even more when Commander Zaja took her to task for voicing such sentiments in public and Amanita began to describe how *warm* and *friendly* and *open* everything is in Aldyrwald. And then Inga joined in with her detached, clinical tone to say that Amanita wasn't wrong – the original builders really *were* going for *intimidating and downtrodden.*

Even though Amanita and I weren't in a great position to listen to her on the ride up, we'd still got to hear most of the story of what happened when the *Líonar* got thrown out of Pathremir and fled down here.

There were a lot more of them, as Inga mentioned yesterday, but they weren't facing scattered family-groups. The indigenous people of Selavan already had a fairly well-established civilization – based on fishing and trade and some agriculture – and they'd been trading *with* the *Líonar* when they ruled Pathremir *(as **Loptheim**)* for the past thousand years. They weren't under any particular illusions about who they were facing.

And... based on the looks on Puck's face, my guess is that they had some warning of what was about to happen beyond what their own spies and traders would have told them.

Now I'm wondering just *how old* Puck *is*.

Anyways, the refugees from Pathremir had to take a different approach when they came down into Selavan. They were still way more war-like than the indigenous Selavani, but they had no resources or supply-lines and they had all their families with them... and they were faced with an organized resistance. So... they negotiated instead of conquering.

Apparently, their leader was able to get himself or his son *(we missed that part)* married to the indigenous Selavani princess and then volunteered his entire people as warriors for the Selavani ruler. And then the princess' *Lionar*-Selavani kid was Chosen by their God, the Lord of Light, to be the next King of Selavan. So, I guess even the royal line *does* have some indigenous blood.

Commander Zaja sent a few of her troop ahead of us to give warning of our arrival, and we were greeted with a reasonable amount of pomp and ceremony *(not like in Calabasha, thank goodness – that was as insanely overdone as the rest of that place)*. Our horses – except for Twinklestar – were taken away and we were guided into the Presence of Their Majesties.

It was sort of funny to watch all the diplomats and nobles scrambling around to figure out how to handle Twinklestar coming in with me *(though not as funny as it had been in Calabasha – they seem more into unicorns here)*.

So... when the Selavani refer to their rulers as 'His Effulgent Majesty' and the 'Luminous Queen' – they aren't being overly dramatic. The king and queen actually *glow.*

I mean, I know how it's *done*, of course. Papa showed me how to add that little extra bit to make it look like you're glowing back when I was ten or eleven. It's not really *useful* most of the time, since who are we going to use it *on?* All the neighbors can do the same things as far as I know. But it's fun to play with.

There's a harder version where it's not so much *looking like* you're glowing, but you actually *bend* the light in whatever space you're in to shine on you a bit more. Still more of a toy than anything, I always thought.

And then there's the actual emitting light, like a candle or a lantern kind of deal. Which is *really* a lot of work, and also *really* not worth it, since if you ever *needed* that kind of thing, one of the other approaches would probably work just as well.

You can tell the difference between the different ways of *glowing* by checking which way the shadows go. If the shadows don't change, it's the first thing. If they point *towards* the person who's *glowy*, it's the second one. And if the shadows point *away* from them, it's the third.

Jo and Roger and Prissy and the other New Gods sort of *glow* the last way all of the time if They aren't paying attention. *(And since it's more work, it usually takes* **more** *attention, not less. Which I suppose is a fairly good argument for them actually being* **Gods** *and not just super-powerful sorcerers. Not that I disbelieve them or anything, but hearing about what happened to those* **Líonar** *dudes when* **their** *Gods faked Their deaths... has got me thinking.)* They can tone it down when They need to, and always look a little embarrassed when it comes up. Prissy says that They have so *much* magickal energy *(or divine energy – She wasn't clear on what the difference is)* pouring off of Them all the time that it's not the usual kind of magickal *glow...* it's more like the visible manifestation of the magick dispersing.

(Or something like that. Cythera – the Fire Goddess, because this came up right after Roger and Joanna's wedding, so She was still visiting – claims that **all** *light is basically something like that. And Roger disagreed and said there's a difference between* **light** *and* **glowing particles** *that are moving through the air...and since He's the Wind God, I guess He would know? And then Cythera started arguing about it and it got all technical and I gave up and went off to do something else.)*

Well, Lochea the Luminous Queen had more of the Joanna-and-Roger kind of *glowing* going on. She seemed to be wrapped in moonlight.

King Mithral... seemed to be doing the hard kind of *glowing* that I could manage if I had to. He held it up for the entire time we were there – which is *way* more than I could do, but he was looking sort of stressed and grim by the end of the formal greetings. And the royal pair left the audience chamber before we were all the way out – and all the torches *(yeah, they're using torches... for 'ambiance,' apparently)* in the room went out when he did.

Amanita – and the rest of the Pathremiri, but especially her and Daffyd – were very impressed with Queen Lochea. Not so much with the king, though my personal thought is that if he's able to put that much work into just *glowing,* he'd be a fairly tough adversary and maybe they should take him a little more seriously.

Though I can see why that's hard.

He's only in his early thirties, I was told, but he *looks* older. Like some of Papa's older knights do: the start of a beer-gut over an otherwise fit frame; bags under his eyes; hair starting to go grey from that startlingly bright golden shade that some of these *Líonar* people have. From where Twinklestar and I stood, it didn't look like his eyes were bloodshot, but... he looked like a man who was too fond of strong drink and starting to lose his battle to keep it under control.

Except not quite.

And every time his Queen spoke and he turned to her, he looked a little better. Healthier, stronger, even *taller* though his posture didn't change like he was trying to impress her. Almost the reverse in some ways. He looked like he *loves* her, but he kind of doesn't want to.

It was... a little weird, to be quite honest.

Anyhow, after the Royal Audience, we were shown to guest rooms in the castle – I have my own here, too, thank the Gods. Supper will be sent up and there will be some sort of entertainments tomorrow afternoon and a ball in the evening.

Twinklestar suffered himself to be taken down to the stables and 'reunited with his beloved Chillabiaen' *(he can be **such** a drama-colt),* so neither the staff nor I had to figure out how to get him through the castle corridors. Nor how to deal with his, ah, *stable-sweepings.* He may be a unicorn, but he has a horse's indifference as to where his droppings go... until he wants to sleep in that space and then it's hell to pay for whomever didn't deal with his mess.

I need to get someone to show me the dances that are popular here before that. All those stultifying dancing lessons Mama made me go through had better come in handy at last!

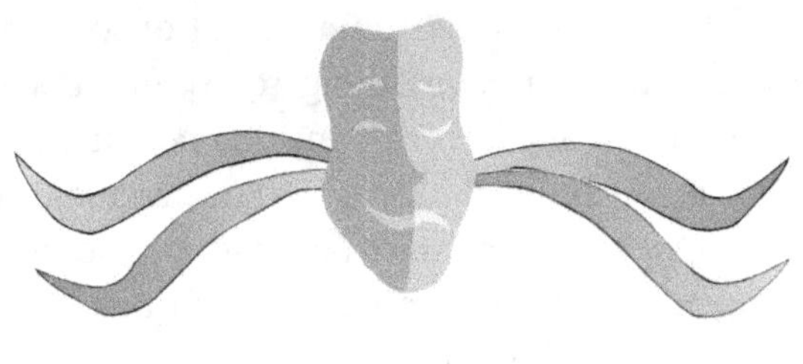

Day 48

'Entertainments' indeed. This afternoon there was some sort of gambling-sport-thing going on in one of the big rooms. People the same age as me and Amanita and Daffyd were betting – and I don't really understand how gambling works, but it didn't take much watching to realize that *most* of them are *losing*. Which makes no sense, since if it's a fair game of chance there should be about even odds, right?

I don't have enough money to take chances on this stuff, so I wandered off to see what else was going on.

There was a room with people playing music on instruments I've never seen before. Most of them were girls, and I got out of there quickly. Their eyes were almost *hungry* and since I've been told there aren't any princesses here besides King Mithral and Queen Lochea's baby daughter... well, there didn't seem to be much point.

The castle's lists were open and a number of young noblemen were trying their swords against each other. I stayed *there* long enough to see that they use a different style *(more chop and bash)* than what Roger and Jeremy were starting to teach me back home.

There was the room where Amanita was the nominal hostess for an afternoon tea – it was supposed to be a meet-and-greet for the visiting royalty, is how it was described. I avoided that room after peeking inside. Amanita was leaning back in an oversized chair with her arms folded, looking like a grumpy princess doll, while Kyrista's sister, Jessina Keetering – who is up here with her fiancé – *actually* acted as a hostess for the people who were there. Inga had gotten roped into staying there and looked about as engaged as Amanita.

Daffyd was there as well, presumably out of some sort of loyalty, but he leaned down to say something to Amanita when he caught sight of me peeking in. She freed a hand to wave irritably at him and glowered in the direction of the door – and, presumably *me*.

Hey, it's not *my* fault that she's being given the 'royal treatment' and I'm getting more or less ignored. Next-but-one in line for the throne of the country's biggest rival/threat vastly outranks Crown Prince of a country no one's ever heard of.

A moment later, Daffyd came out of the room and joined me.

"Commander Zaja told her *three times* before all this stuff started," he waved a hand to indicate the 'entertainments,' "that she's lucky they're treating her with the respect due her rank. A couple years ago, before the king and queen were wed and Selavan started changing its attitudes, *I'd* be the one they're fawning over and they'd have ignored *her* entirely."

"I think she might prefer that," I replied. "I take it the tea is not going well."

Daffyd shook his head. "Women are being taken more seriously here since Queen Lochea's crowning, but it's still not 'normal' for them. So, the room is filled with gossipy wives of noblemen and their giddy daughters."

"And they're all full-blooded *Líonar,*" I noted. "Which probably isn't helping."

Daffyd sighed, agreed, and then suggested we figure out where Puck had gotten to.

Puck – or rather *Prince Skiftglow* – had apparently been wandering in circles like me, but we'd managed not to run into each other. When we caught up with him, he was in the gaming room and his eyes were gleaming as he watched the dice roll.

We gathered him up and got him out of there rather quickly.

The God of Pranksters – and *Chance* – in a room full of gamblers? How could *that* possibly go well?

"Do they know who *you* are?" I asked him. "For real, I mean?"

Puck gave me a raised eyebrow. "In what sense? I really *am* Prince Skiftglow, you know. Though I haven't used that name much for a very long while."

I rolled my eyes. "Do they know Who your Mother is?"

He shrugged nonchalantly. "You heard the herald announce me. It's no great secret."

"They introduced you as 'Prince Skiftglow, son of Queen Snowmistral of the Snow-Fairies'," I pointed out. "Do they not know what other Name She goes by? Or Who else *you* are?"

Puck shrugged again. "Mother hasn't really had all that much to do with what goes on over on this side of the Misty Mountains, Thony. I wouldn't be surprised if even the *Líonar* don't remember Her over here, and the rest of the Selavani have never had anything to do with Her at all. She's the Lady of *Mountain*-Breezes after all."

"And you?" I persisted. "Pranksters are ubiquitous."

He sighed. "Not so much as you might think. Selavan... has tended to take itself a bit too seriously in *my* opinion."

Daffyd snorted. "*Both* of my grandmothers would probably prefer if Pathremir saw less of you in that capacity. Amanita was a handful since she was *born*."

For a brief instant, I would *swear* that Puck's face was bleak and distraught... but then he had his usual, ah, *puckish* expression. "Are you so sure about that? Namarina was a fair handful herself at one point as I recall. And Reyalla is always stirring up *some* kind of trouble."

Daffyd looked like he wanted to agree and disagree both. I guess he settled on the disagree part – he's much more loathe to criticize his grandmothers than Amanita. Or any women. Survival tactic growing up in Pathremir, I suppose. "Grandmother-the-*Queen* was a handful? I can't believe that. She's always so stately and wise and..."

He paused, possibly remembering something that didn't quite fit those descriptions, to guess by his face.

Puck grinned. "Oh, she was *more* than a *handful,* gran– lad. She was a beautiful, reckless young princess that neither your mother nor your sister has quite managed to top for wildness and daring. Despite their own bloodline. Or yours, for that matter. Speaking of people who are too serious most of the time."

Which was surely saying something, since Amanita had so far run away through the Fairy Wood and helped stop a war.

There was also something weird about the way Puck said that. It was almost as if he had started to call Daffyd... nah, that must have been my imagination. Scratch all that.

Daffyd lifted his chin. "*You* try growing up a boy in Pathremir, Puck. Wildness is *not* rewarded."

And the Snow-Fairy Prince actually winced at that. "Yes, well..."

"And I *still* don't believe you about Grandmother." Daffyd rolled his eyes. "*Especially* not compared to Amanita. You can*not* tell me that *Grandmother* ran off and crossed the Fairy Wood at twelve-years-old for no better reason than a whim."

Hunh. I wonder if *Daffyd* doesn't know that Amanita left partly to protect *him*. Interesting.

"Your mother had her wild moments, too," Puck had a sort of look of fond remembrance. "And no, neither of them crossed the Wood. They had... other adventures. Ask them when you get home. And tell them that I said if *they* tell you, *I* won't."

Daffyd gave him a confused look, but something else had caught my attention.

"When *he* gets home? Aren't you coming with us to Queen Namarina's Court?"

And that brief look of almost *brilliant* sadness passed over Puck's face *again*. "It's probably better for everyone if I don't." He paused. "My Mother's Realm is farther up the mountains anyways."

And, *that* was disheartening news. Amanita and Daffyd are going to be subsumed in official duties once we get back, I'm sure. I had hoped to have at least *one* friend still around who would have time for me.

The 'entertainments' ended shortly thereafter and everyone retired to change clothes *again* and eat dinner privately before the ball. They don't seem to like banquets at this Court – not that I mind. Figuring out table manners in different Courts is really *not* a top ambition for me.

I managed to get the attention of one of the butlers and explained my concern about dancing. He said he'd send a dancing-instructor up to help me out during the break and – whoops! There's the door.

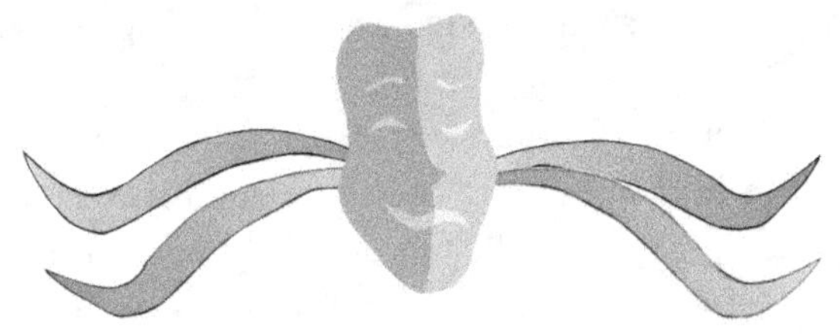

Day 48 – late night
(early morning of Day 49)

Well, the ball wasn't *too* bad of a disaster in terms of the dancing.

The dancing-instructor turned out to be a grumpy old lady with the most *perfect* posture I have ever seen. She brought along a chamber music quartet for us to practice to. She was quite the martinet – in two hours I had five different dances step-perfect, even by her standards.

She left with a final instruction that I should commend my previous instructor for providing a solid base. I'm sure Mama and what's-his-name will both be pleased if and when I ever can do that.

I danced with Jessina Keetering and met her fiancé, the *Líonar* nobleman, Torsthyn Danessen. He seemed nice, but kind of boring the way people in love often do. You know, all googly-eyed at Jessina and not really paying attention to much else. I gather their engagement is relatively new.

And I danced with Inga, which went very well. I hadn't been sure, given that she seems incredibly uninterested in anything other than books. But I suppose she's gotten stuck with the same kinds of lessons I did.

I even got to dance with the Queen.

More interesting was watching Amanita and Queen Lochea meet up close.

The Queen was very interested and Amanita was trying very hard *not* to be.

I couldn't overhear their conversation, of course. The only way to do that would have been to stick around to have Amanita as my next partner and after watching her stomp on everyone's toes from her brother to King Mithral, there was *no way* I was dancing with her.

(Later on, Puck told me she didn't stomp on **his** *toes, so apparently, it's a choice – like how she makes herself look frumpy in a gown until* **she** *decides not to. I'm still glad I didn't take the chance. It's not like* **Daffyd** *had done anything to end her up here, and if she was willing to stomp on the toes of the king of the country hers has been on-and-off at war with for thousands of years... who's to say she wouldn't decide to mash mine as well?)*

(Though I guess you have to admire her moxy for daring to step on the king's toes.)

Daffyd partnered Inga three times that I saw, so I think *he* was trying to avoid his sister as well. And all those Selavani noblewomen who are not anywhere *near* as modest as the girls back home. My ears were burning after I danced with any of *them*.

Well, other than Inga, of course.

I'm using the next page or so to write down a list of all the books I can still remember that Inga recommended to me during the one piece that we danced to.

- *Keladrynn the Eternal King: Founder of Taridawil*
- *Tales of the Turquoise Empire: The Great Pirate Disaster*
- *The Light of Aura* (this one is a romance, but she says it's tragic, so it might not be too lame)
- *(Nearly) Ten Millennia – Lessons to be learned from the Turquoise Empire*
- *Falling Down a Well: Humorous Tales of (unintended) Travels in the Fairy Wood*
- *The Artha Shastra* (she suggested this one and another one to help me figure out how to deal with the neighbors back in Aldyrwald)

Darn... I know there were more... I'll have to try to catch her tomorrow and ask.

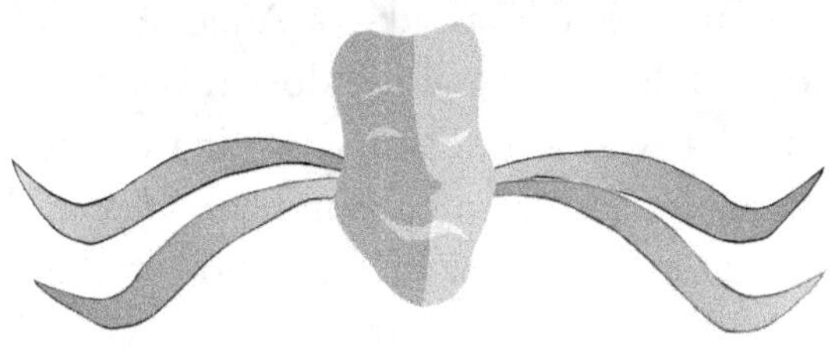

Day 49

I'm realizing that while there is a lot going on at this Court, I don't think I really missed out on anything by not traveling around the Mountain-Region the way I used to beg Papa to let me do. This is a much bigger Court because Selavan is a much bigger country than Aldyrwald, but otherwise things are all about the same.

I was going to skip out on today's afternoon 'entertainment' – a hunt – because my skills with a bow are even worse than my skills with a sword. Shooting from horseback is *not* to be imagined.

But Puck explained that with forty or so nobles on the hunt hardly anyone is actually going to get to make a shot on target for whatever the huntsmen flush for us. So, my skills are almost irrelevant.

I checked with Twinklestar and he wasn't interested, so I 'borrowed' back Silverfoot from Amanita. *(He's **my** horse, after all.)*

It was sort of fun – Mama and Papa never let me go on hunts – but it was also boring.

I mean, the scenery was pretty and all *(which I noticed once I was clear that we were pretty far from any cliffs and stopped worrying about all of us accidentally riding off of one of them)*, but I'd just really get started looking around when someone would shout that the deer had been spotted and we'd all push our steeds to a gallop for a couple minutes. And having a conversation with any of the other young men was about as possible as looking at the scenery.

I did it without Puck *or* Daffyd – or Amanita, since women don't hunt here though I don't know if she does this sort of thing at home anyways – and that was a little scary. Jessina's fiancé, Torsthyn, let me keep up with him so I wasn't around *complete* strangers. I heard later that he often manages a successful shot on these things – so it was awfully nice of him to stay with me, since I stayed near the back of the group. Unfamiliar ground for me and Silverfoot and all.

It got a little *weird* heading back up after we bagged a few deer. The other guys seemed to think I'd done a fair job of keeping up – and they think Silverfoot is a pretty good horse. So, they actually talked to me and wanted to know about Raven'sWing's invasion and stuff. I don't think they believed me when I told them that it was our prank-campaign that set things up so our side could win, but they loved hearing about some of the pranks themselves.

I may have planted a few ideas. Puck might find this place getting a bit more lively.

They *also* had a great deal of fun telling me about which of their sisters and cousins and whatnot kept talking about me and Daffyd at breakfast. Daffyd is '*dark* and *exotic*' and has that cachet of being a prince of their ancient enemy. But apparently, *I* look enough like a *Líonar* that some of them started really quizzing me about Aldyrwald and my ancestors. Like their sisters and whatnot were *interested* enough that I might be hearing from their fathers.

Which, I suppose could work out if any of their fathers have warriors to send along with. I mean… it's not like anyone at home is going to check on whether the girl I bring home really is a princess. And if a Worthy Miller's Daughter is good enough *(with the appropriate quest on her part)*, to be a princess-consort, surely the daughter of a… a duke or a count or something should work out.

So long as she comes with a fighting force. Or the credible threat of one.

I wonder if Count Einirsgeld has any sworn knights. Inga is the least annoying girl here.

The guys in the hunting party were satisfyingly sympathetic about my need to bring home a bride who comes with allies. And satisfyingly dismayed to hear about my bride-assassin problem.

They seemed a little baffled when the phrase 'middleborn' came up, though. Not a Thing here, I guess.

Which makes me wonder why it is at home.

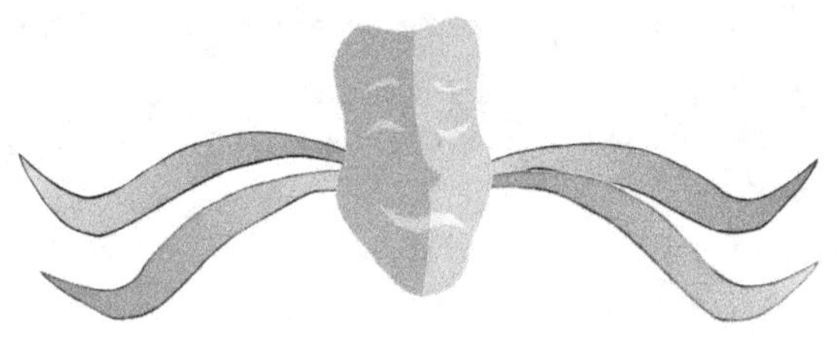

Day 49

(late night/early morning... again)

There was another ball tonight.

Amanita was in a better mood – pensive instead of irritated – so I dared to dance with her. My toes survived.

I'm not sure what changed. We haven't had a chance to talk since we got here.

I never got a chance to dance with Inga. Every time I looked, Daffyd was either dancing with her or talking to her.

The older ladies kept me moving tonight, though. As a foreign prince, I'm supposed to take a turn around the floor with each of the top-ranked ladies at least once. Or sit out a piece with some of the oldest ladies *(which is, frankly, a relief)*. I've now danced with every one of King Mithral's female relatives or relations-by-marriage out to the third degree, I think.

I'm also getting caught up on the local gossip *(the old ladies are particularly good with that)*.

Apparently Istevan used to *pretend* to be a foreign prince *(from some place way off west called Ilseador)* at this Court. He was really being a spy for some duke who is now in utter disgrace, though not because of the spying and – or so the king's aunt-by-marriage assured me with a very odd expression – not even for *framing* other nobles who threatened his power and getting them either disgraced or executed. *(I got the impression that her husband was one of the people who got framed.)*

No, the duke is in disgrace for opposing His Majesty's marriage to Queen Lochea.

About half their priesthood was defrocked for opposing the marriage as well.

Because King Mithral – and they've mentioned this before, but I sort of thought it was some kind of ceremonial thing – is the Chosen Disciple of the Lord of Light. And Queen Lochea is the Chosen Disciple of *both* the Lord of Light *and* the Goddess of Light and Dark.

And the *Gods* decided they had to be married. *(Which might explain the odd way he was looking at her when we first arrived.)*

And this disgraced duke – Duke Alfspar – *might* also have been angling for the throne. He's a cousin of the king himself – from the *salic* side, which normally wouldn't fly, but he'd managed to get most of the king's closer male relatives disqualified one way or another and they're still trying to sort all that out. It kind of left Duke Alfspar – or his sons, because King Mithral is younger than the duke – as the next in line for the throne.

And it sounded like there was even darker stuff going on, but the way the old lady was hinting, she probably doesn't know either.

She seemed quite pleased to have Amanita and Daffyd here, though. All the older ladies had good things to say about the new peace with Pathremir and their own new Queen and how that's improving things for the status of women in Selavan.

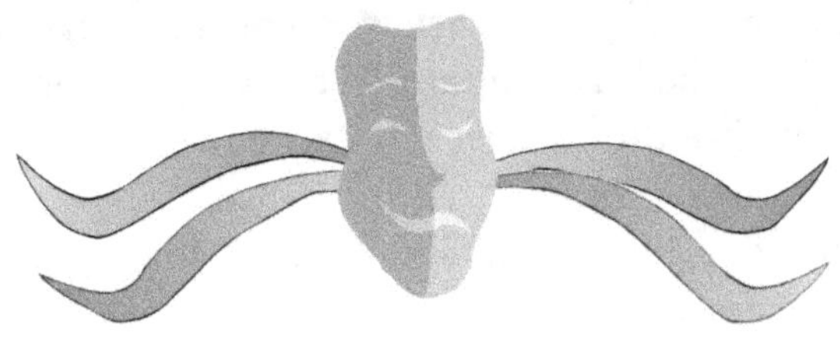

Day 50

I know we've only been here for three and a half days, but... it feels a lot longer.

I never thought I'd say it, but I kind of miss being on the road. Even with Commander Zaja and her grim-faced women-warriors.

(Okay, the younger ones aren't so grim-faced, but they still aren't up for making friends with me.)

I finally got to talk to Amanita – last night when we were dancing together, we plotted out meeting over breakfast. This was harder than it sounds, given that we're staying up past midnight at these balls – which is a *lot* of work. Dancing sounds easy, but it is *not*.

She says that Queen Lochea's 'Goddess of Light and Dark' is her own Silver Dragon Goddess. Though they aren't using Her Name or other titles. The Selavani are used to not having a proper Name for their Lord of Light and they still have a lot of negative stories about dragons *(ah ha!* **This** *is where the dragons-as-bad-guys can be found!)* so it seems wiser not to let everyone in on how their new Goddess is really a dragon.

Or *sometimes* the Goddess is a dragon.

Amanita says I'm probably going to meet Her and then I'll see what she means.

Yay me.

And Selavan is in the middle of some ginormous theological crisis in addition to all the other stuff.

I had thought Daffyd and Puck were going to join us for breakfast, but they both ditched. Amanita didn't know why either. She agrees this place takes itself too seriously – except for all the vapid girls she keeps getting stuck with.

This afternoon I hunted down the castle library. After Dauntless it was... rather disappointing.

Also, Daffyd and Inga were in there and she was using a 'teaching voice,' so I left again.

I ran into Puck right outside the library – he had this rather bemused expression, but he was up for giving me a sword lesson. It didn't go *too* badly, considering that I haven't even tried anything since leaving home like three months ago. Thank the... um, thank goodness they had wooden practice swords handy – Puck agreed that I probably shouldn't go near edged steel for awhile.

Actually, he told me to avoid sharp things entirely. Sigh.

No ball tonight, so maybe I can catch up on sleep some.

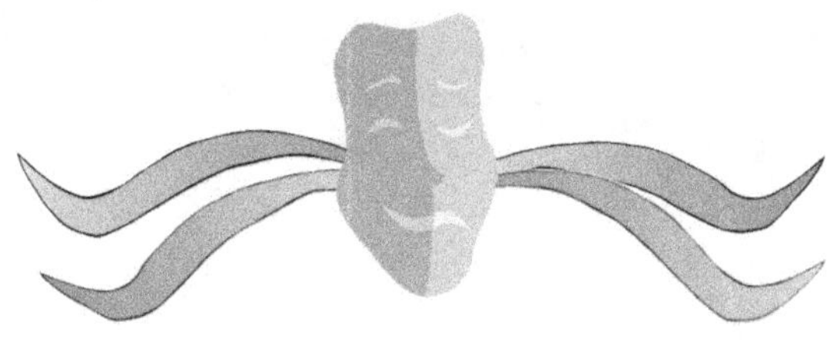

Day 51

since leaving Flowerdust

And we were in Flowerdust for about a month.

So that puts me at nearly a *season* since I left home.

My birthday is long gone. I totally missed it in all the excitement and busy.

If I were in Aldyrwald, I'd be married by now.

Or dead.

This is not quite the adventures that I thought I'd be doing.

Though I suppose dealing with Raven'sWing's invasion was pretty cool. In retrospect.

At the time it was just scary and exhausting.

I miss Mama.

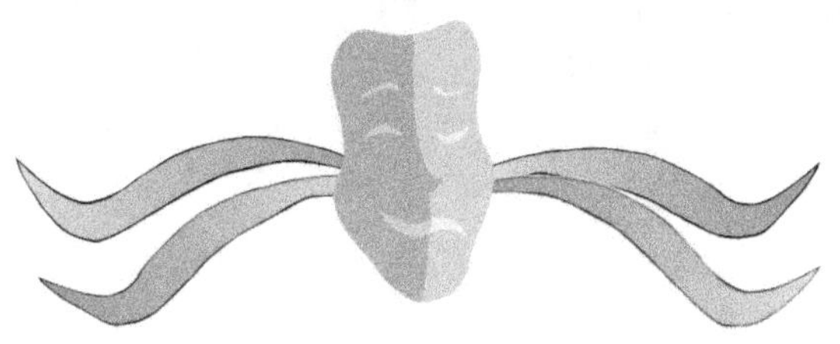

Day 52

My sword-lessons with Puck have continued. Some of the other young noblemen have joined in, so I'm learning some of what they do up here in Selavan, too. I don't think it's a style that works terribly well for me, since it's all about being more powerful than your opponent and I'm still pretty dinky-sized, but it's probably good for me to learn how to defend against it.

Daffyd hasn't joined us, despite Puck trying pretty hard to interest him. That might be because Commander Zaja gives him dark looks and makes him wilt every time it comes up.

Neither has Amanita, despite her being bored out of her mind. I think it's because Commander Zaja is trying pretty hard to get *her* to be interested in sword-stuff.

But it might be because of that *and* because the commander is being mean to Daffyd about it.

She can be complicated when she wants to. Which is most of the time.

There was another hunt this afternoon. We brought back 2 deer and a whole family of partridges.

Daffyd and Amanita didn't come for that, either.

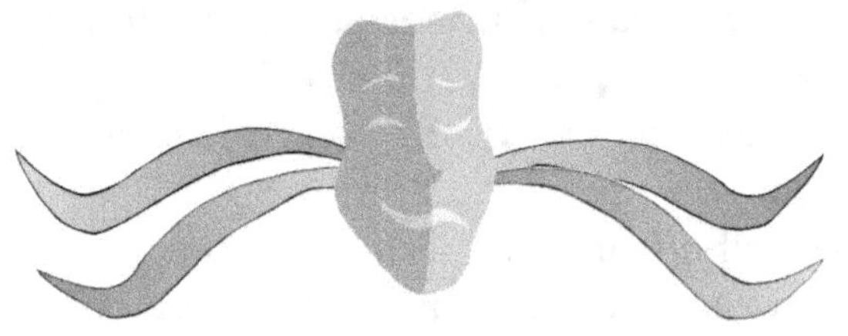

Day 53

While I'm not sure what the point of staying here is, I'm starting to make a few friends among the young noblemen. I never had guy-friends of my age who were also close to my rank back at home, so this is different.

Of course, I never had *any* friends other than my sisters *(and their husbands, so they don't count either)* until Amanita and Wes.

Wow. I haven't even thought about Wes in ages.

I wonder what he's doing.

I wonder what my parents and my sisters are doing.

I hope nobody has invaded Aldyrwald. My leaving was supposed to make it look like Roger *(as Joanna's husband)* was now Papa's Heir. Which *we* all know he can't be, because he's busy being a God, but the neighbors don't. And Roger's dad, King Richie, might be a jerk but I didn't think he'd let his middleborn-son-who-managed-to-make-good get invaded. After all, Roger ruling Aldyrwald would extend Schwannsberg's influence.

And even if King Richie wasn't going to be cool, Roger's brothers still care about him. And Raymond *(the older one)* can probably see that their dad's attitudes are dumb.

I hope.

I *really* hope, because I'm not any closer to finding a princess than I was last week.

I inquired delicately *(at least I hope it was delicately)* about the Einirsgeld family.

They are well-off, and well-regarded... but they don't have sworn knights or anything. And Inga has half a dozen older siblings who need dowries and stuff, so she's not getting much.

(That kind of surprised me, actually. In the Mountain-Region the oldest and youngest get dowered, but the middleborns don't, since no one is going to marry them anyways. And really only the daughters, since the princes are either inheriting or going off to find an heiress. It makes it more affordable to have these large families, I suppose.)

I hate having to look at things this way – she's really nice, and even if she's way older than me, she's way younger than any of the middleborn princesses I might be offered back home. And she wouldn't want to kill me. And she's a youngest, so that would be something. And I might have been able to bribe her with the idea of using the Aldyrwald treasury to build a library.

Though, come to think of it, I don't know if she cares if the peasants learn to read or not.

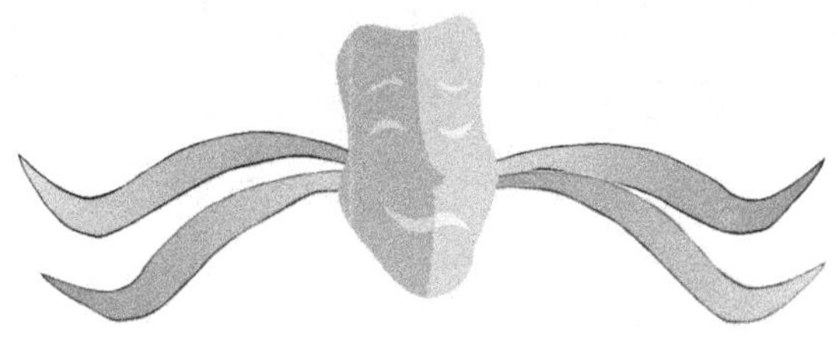

Day 54

Well, my 'delicate inquiries' *were* noticed.

Just, it seems like everyone assumed I was asking on behalf of Daffyd, who *has* been spending just about every waking minute with her, to be fair.

My impression has been that she's been bringing him up to speed on all the history of Pathremir and Selavan and the *Líonar* and the original Mistlanders and all. I gather there are a great many more details than she and Kyrista told the rest of us.

I'm pretty sure that's all Inga is thinking about it.

I'm not so sure about Daffyd.

And now – and it's all my fault – Inga's parents are noticing how much time they're spending together. And they *don't* look happy.

Clearly, it's my duty *(and privilege)* to fix this.

At least coming up with something that will distract everyone should alleviate some of the boring. *(I never knew before that you could be super-busy and also bored.)*

I wonder if Amanita will want to help.

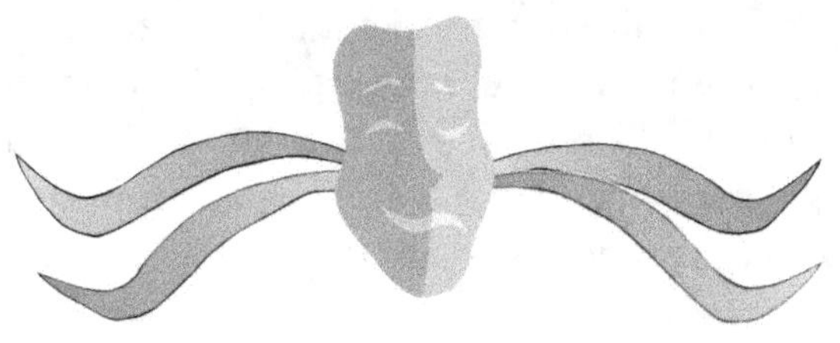

Day 55

It has been way too long since I have put a real prank together. I feel rusty.

Though at least I'm not bored anymore.

On reflection, I decided *not* to bring Amanita in on this. She tends to go a little overboard anyways and since she has this generational grudge she's carrying for... basically everyone around us... it seemed like things might get a little out of hand if she's involved.

And Puck... seems oddly distracted and serious.

There's Daffyd himself, of course, but then I'd have to explain *why* I'm doing this. And he got all judgy and big-brothery the times Amanita and I were reminiscing about pranks. Also, since the point is to distract everyone from how he and Inga have been spending time together, setting anything up so that he ends up getting *more* attention is probably not wise.

Frogs are kind of my go-to for casual pranks... but I haven't seen any good frog habitats in the castle environs *(we're on top of a rocky cliff after all)* and it's not going to be easy to collect frogs when I'm out with a hunting party.

Actually, they keep us busy enough that it's hard to find planning and setup time *at all*.

Hunh.

Maybe that's on purpose.

Well, anyways, this would be an ideal situation to set something up by starting a rumor... Except these people have turned gossip into an artform and backstabbing into... hmmmn. Another artform. I couldn't possibly compete with what they already have going...

I'll need to think about this a little more...

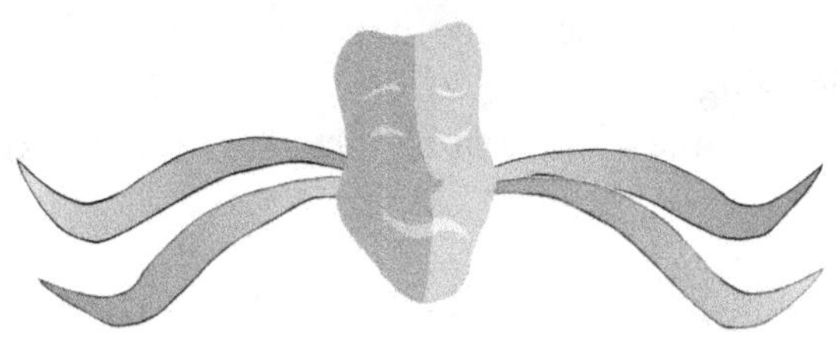

Day 60

Well... I didn't think there was much point for us staying at King Mithral's Court...

But I also didn't mean to get us kicked out.

Or, um, asked to *please leave. NOW.*

I think Queen Lochea thought it was funny.

I *know* Jessina Keetering did. And her fiancé, Torsthyn Danessen, didn't even bother to hide his smirks. Neither did a lot of the young men I'd been hunting with... well, the ones who weren't directly involved anyways.

Amanita is annoyed, and Commander Zaja is *livid.*

I have been instructed *not to talk* until we are past Dynsfyor.

And *no,* I may not visit Dauntless as we depart.

If I am *very* good, she *might* let me bid Madame Keetering and Mister Keetering a proper goodbye.

There's a sort of threat hovering about how much worse everything will get once we make it actually *into* Pathremir.

I'm considering running away *(again).*

Anyways, I suppose I might as well put down all the details, since I've been locked into a room *(with a couple of the girl-guards at the door... outside **and in. Both.)** until we're ready to leave.

First, I want it to be clear that Commander Zaja is *seriously* overblowing things.

I mean, everyone's hair will be the same colors that it used to be in a few days.

A week, tops.

In a month it'll be something they all laugh at.

Maybe in a year they'll start appreciating my ingenuity in getting dyes everywhere in almost-perfect synchronicity. *(Hey, it's a big castle – more of a compound, even. There was no way I could get things to **really** be simultaneous all on my own.)*

You have to appreciate how very *grey* it is here to really understand.

The castle is made of grey stone. The cliffs are grey – and there's no dirt or flowers or trees until down by the village. *(They call it the 'service village,' since that's where all the servants live and do the tasks that they don't want done actually up in the castle... stuff like, oh, **dyeing** and **soap-making**...).*

Even the *sky* is grey a lot of the time.

The people wear colors, of course, and there's furnishings, but there's this tradition that any room the king might enter has to have unlit torches for the only lighting. Because the torches are supposed to be lit by his presence alone. And they're supposed to go out when he leaves.

Which is sort of hard on him, because that means he has to be using magick *All The Time,* and it also means there's a lot of smoke everywhere and half the rooms and corridors are dark.

So... the place was just begging for some color, right?

Some *local color,* I might even say. I mean, I had to source everything locally, so why not?

There was a great deal of missed sleep involved, since I had to sneak down to the service village a bunch of times to obtain the dyes. And then to find the soap-making area and figure out how to mix the dyes in without anyone noticing.

There's some special things you can do to dyes – a lot of them change color depending on how acidic the solution is that they're in. With some of them, the color-change is heat-triggered. And there's a few other things like that. If you set it up right, you can make it look like there's no dye at all until something special happens. Like, say, hot water being added.

I figured out how to do all of this back at home ages ago, though I hadn't actually *used* the knowledge before for a prank.

One, I hate to repeat pranks; and two, well, there hadn't been the right opportunity.

Anyways, I managed to get into the latest delivery of soap to the castle.

That included bath soap, hand soap, dish soap, laundry soap, and shampoo. They all come from the same base, after all. The real key was discovering that there's a Mistress of Soaps up at the castle who takes the basic flaky stuff that they produce down in the village *(with lye and fat and all – the smelly, messy process that they don't want up at the castle)* and she does stuff with it to make it into all the different kinds of soap used in the castle.

The trick was in getting different specially treated dyes into the different batches. So, all the shampoo had green in it, for example, and all the laundry had red. The baths turned yellow, and the dishes blue. *(Hand soap is basically dish soap, so that was blue, too.)*

The idea was for everything to be sort of alarming in an innocuous but not-entirely-unexpected way. Like, bathwater turning yellow would be gross, but not weird, like if it was purple.

And blonde hair *(like most of these people have)* takes green really well.

And if they just use bath soap instead of shampoo, their hair is a particularly brilliant golden now. *(Which I would have **thought** they'd appreciate.)*

Red hair seems to not take the green terribly well, except at the tips, so the other redheads and I all have green tips and look pretty festive.

You can tell who uses what to wash their hair now. *(Not bathe, though. The dyes don't take well to skin. Erm... mostly, anyways.)*

There were a few snafus, I'll admit. Though why the Dowager Duchess of Heidelkill uses laundry soap to wash her hair, I have no idea. And a surprising number of people use dish soap.

Queen Lochea looks really pretty with green hair. I'd say she looks like a dryad, but that half-dryad girl from Eyola – Midele – didn't have green hair at all. *(Maybe if her hair hadn't been so dark, it would have been greenish? I wonder what her mom looks like.)*

King Mithral, on the other hand, apparently used some hand soap as well as his shampoo. My guess is that he rubbed his hands through his wet hair without completely rinsing them. And... that the towel he dried off with had gotten some laundry soap sprinkled on it.

His hair is a rather demonic-looking mix of green and blue with spots of red mixed in.

He was *not* amused.

So, with half the ladies of his Court weeping and the other half seething... he had to do *something*. And when he had the Mistress of Soaps dragged into the audience hall, I couldn't let her take the credi– er, the blame.

Which is what led to us being kicked out.

Commander Zaja was aghast at my behavior.

Honestly, it's like she didn't listen to any of the stories from Flowerdust at all. Like how the pranks Amanita and Dae and I *(and Jost's crew)* played made Puck strong enough to break the magick barrier that Valderon Raven'sWing and Shalladra Stillheart had placed over that grove of the Fairy Wood. Which is what won the war, because then Lady Opalsinger and Lord Aspenheart could come out and finish the job.

I mean, this is what I *do*.

Oh, it looks like we're ready to leave.

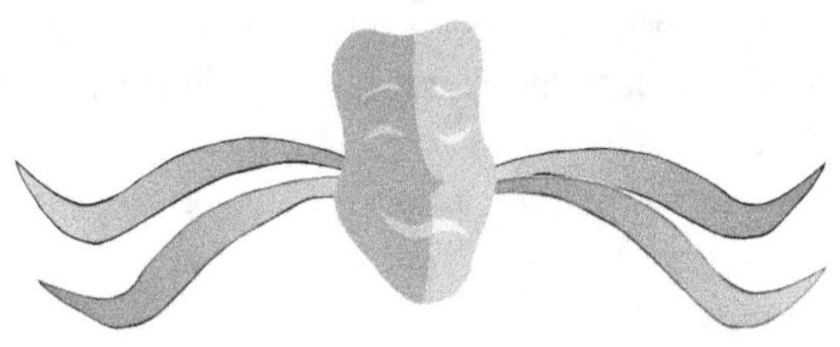

Day 66

So... I'm still in bad odor with just about everyone.

Including Twinklestar, it turns out, since apparently, they use a mix of dish soap and laundry soap on the horses up there... And since he's, um, *normally* a fairly glisteny white he's now...

Well, a rather glisteny mix of purple, blue and red.

I think it looks rather spectacular on him – and I liked it even better when it turned out that my stupid unicorn-maiden *robe* automatically matches him. I absolutely *love* this new look.

And I think Twinklestar will get over it once he realizes Chillabiaen is giving him rather interested looks as well. I mean, she's *Puck's* steed, so this is probably fairly tame stuff to her.

In the meantime, however, he is punishing me with an even worse gait than normal.

And Amanita is mad and not talking to me.

And Daffyd isn't talking to me. *(Or anyone else, actually.)*

And Commander Zaja is avoiding even *looking* at me. *(Which is actually an improvement.)*

At least the troop is sort of snickering over the whole thing *(when their commander isn't paying attention)*. None of *their* hair-color got changed, since it's so dark already. And their clothes somehow ended up a very even and attractive shade of red. They seem to like it better than the usual tans and browns of their traveling leathers.

And Puck isn't *mad* at me – even though *his* hair *is* green – but he seems worried about Daffyd and is spending all his time trying to get him to talk.

I was allowed to say good bye to the Keeterings when we passed through Dynsfyor. Madame Keetering even gave me a hug *(for which Commander Zaja scolded me afterwards, saying I deserved absolutely **no** sympathy)*, and they both looked like they were trying not to laugh.

Jessina and her fiancé, Torsthyn, had stayed up at the castle with Inga and her parents *(and his parents)*. Inga had waved at us when we left – she seemed a little baffled by the whole fuss, but I don't think she cares about looks. Jessina's hair is so pale and thin that it took the dye very strongly and she looks like she's part willow tree, but Tor seemed to think she was just as pretty as ever.

So, there are at least a few people who aren't mad at me.

Just... none of the ones who are *with* me.

(Except for Puck.)

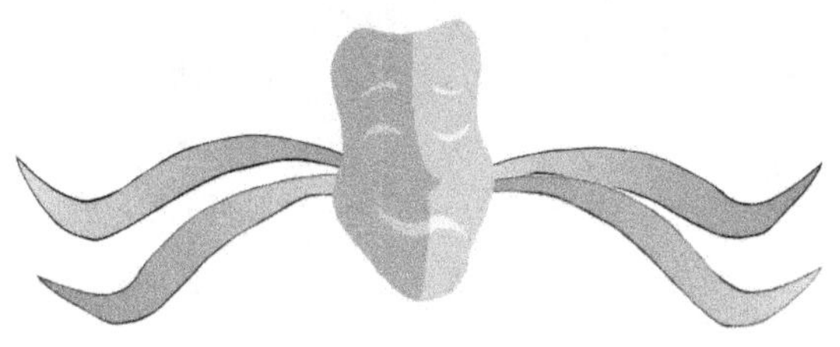

Day 70

This silent treatment is really starting to suck.

The troop isn't mad at me, but they've been told not to talk to me.

Amanita *won't*.

Daffyd still seems not to want to talk to *anybody*.

Puck talks to me a little bit, but is still focusing on Daffyd.

At least Twinklestar seems to have given up on trying to punish me – my guess is that keeping up that awkward, jouncy gait is nearly as hard on him as it is on me. He still won't talk to me, though.

And I've been forbidden by Commander Zaja to even talk to the staff at the inns we're staying in, so I can't even request a soak in a hot bath after all of Twinklestar's revenge.

The good news is that after *days* of miserable riding... my muscles are getting used to it and I'm *less* sore.

Yeah, that's the good news.

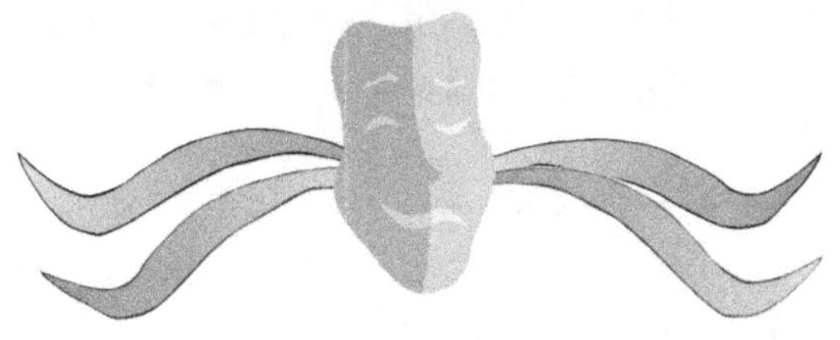

Day 75

We are finally all the way into Pathremir.

The mountain passes were... not great. Even if it felt good not to be the tallest thing around *(other than buildings and horses and the occasional trees)*. I think I was down on the plains too long and it mucked with my head.

Either that, or maybe these mountains are a lot higher than at home. I've heard of mountain-sickness before, but I've never seen anyone who had it, since Aldyrwald is pretty central to the Mountain-Region and anyone who suffered from it turned back long before reaching us. And I certainly never expected to *feel* it myself.

Ugh.

How *embarrassing*. I'm the Crown Prince of a *mountain country*.

At least my discomfort was mild *(though I had some pretty crazy dreams the night we stopped at the top of the pass)*. I could pretend it all away. And now that we're on the plateau, it all seems fine.

Amanita is talking to me again.

This is a mixed blessing.

Apparently, the problem was that I went ahead and did the prank without getting her to help. I sort of guessed that, but it took her nearly a week to actually break down and tell me. I'd say she's forgiven me, but I don't think she really knows what that means. We're 'moving forwards,' anyways, and 'putting it behind us.'

Those are her phrases, and I'm not going to mess with any of it.

I did have to promise that I will not leave her out of any future pranks I pull.

I added the caveat 'as long as we're in the same place' and she didn't argue, but she looked a little sad. I suppose it was a reminder that although I've come with them to Pathremir, I don't intend to stay super long.

Daffyd is talking to people again – even me. At least they didn't make us share a room on the way up here. Because between his being mad and the, ah, *other thing* it would have been beyond awkward.

Instead, Commander Zaja asked Puck if Daffyd could stay with *him,* and locked me into my room each night. Which was great – so I tried to act like it was a terrible punishment.

I mean, I didn't like being locked in, but there was always a window, and the first thing I checked when they locked me in was how easy it would be to get out if I wanted to.

The answer was always *very,* and I became a little more paranoid about unwanted nocturnal visitors than about being trapped. Nothing ever *happened,* but I boobytrapped the window each night and took my trap down again the next morning before I was allowed out.

Going up and then down the mountains was a lot more work than I had anticipated. Again, ridiculous for the prince of a mountain country, but how was *I* supposed to know, when Mama and Papa insisted I stay in sight of the castle at all times?

And... the complaints I was – well, more *thinking* than *saying* – about the difficulty of the mountains are now biting me in the butt, because Pathremir is *flat.*

Like, really, *really* flat.

Even flatter than the Central Plains is my guess.

Amanita looked a little sheepish when I mentioned this and piled her mashed potatoes all around the edges of her plate to demonstrate the geography of Pathremir. *(Which wasn't really helpful now that we're **here** and I can **see** it for myself. And got Commander Zaja scolding us for playing with our food.)*

It's also not very foggy.

She explained that it *used* to be. *(In legendary times, so who knows for real?)*

The *Líonar (yep, it all comes back to her favorite people)* introduced agriculture, and that changed how the land works, so there aren't as many swamps and stuff, so there's less mist. *(I could swear she said before that she **didn't** know why it's not so misty anymore... is she just seizing the opportunity to blame more stuff on them?)*

Which is partly why the Mist-Maidens – the ones who weren't part-human – left.

Which is why she doesn't like Puck's mom a great deal. Snow-Fairies are just Mist-Maidens in the Winter-time, apparently, and she feels like Queen Snowmistral – a.k.a. the Goddess of Blizzards and Gales – abandoned her people as much as the Silver Dragon did, and for less reason. *(And they still get blizzards and stuff, so that 'abandonment' didn't really have **any** upsides, it looks like.)*

It might make sense, but Selavan and Dysacha were very *different* places than home or Flowerdust and the Central Plains towns.

Pathremir – so far – seems a lot like the Central Plains towns, just a lot less dry and you can see mountains in the distance almost every which way you look. *(I have been assured there are still mountains in the directions where we can't see them, they're just farther away.)*

I hadn't really appreciated the differences between a plateau and a high mountain valley before.

Sigh.

I miss home.

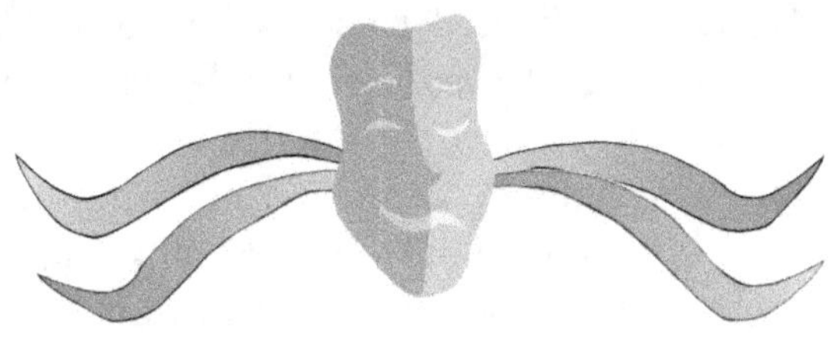

Day 76

I had not fully appreciated where I am until today.

There are mostly women out in the streets of the towns we ride through.

There are *only* women running the shops and inns.

The men I do see all walk around with their eyes cast down... and with a woman nearby them. They don't have leashes, but they act like giant pets. Like those big, drooly dogs that will fall all over themselves for you to pet them.

And they won't *talk* to anyone they don't know – even another guy.

They're more modestly dressed than elsewhere, too. It's all these tent-like robes and headscarves or even facial veils *(at least some of them)* and so on. Except for the guys out working in the fields or at other hard labor – apparently, they can take their shirts and robes off to do that.

The women have a lot more variety in the way they dress, but most of it seems to involve skirts unless they're doing more physical labor. Their dresses are pretty elaborate in some cases, even for what I would otherwise categorize as 'peasants.'

So much for my guess that Amanita's preference for pants was cultural. Although she does seem to like to do more physical stuff, so maybe it still makes sense.

The locals are all delighted to see Amanita and the warriors, cautiously pleased to see Daffyd, baffled by Puck and more than slightly disapproving of me.

Twinklestar says that's because he (and therefore my unicorn-maiden *robe*) are both still slightly spotted pink and purple instead of that absolutely pristine, sparkling white. *I think it's just that they disapprove of men who don't wear tents for clothes or refuse to meet their eyes.*

Also, it's been rather driven home to me that I look rather more like one of those *Lionar*-guys than like Amanita's people. Like village-people everywhere, most of them probably never leave home more than visiting the next village over, so I don't imagine they've seen too many strangers... and I look enough like the guys from the stories they tell their kids to scare the kids into good behavior that I probably freak them all out. *(I know this because Amanita kind of told me about it.)*

It's annoying.

It occurred to me that I could fix some of that by dyeing my hair black or brown – and maybe even darkening my skin a little so I don't stand out so much. *(Can't do anything about my eyes being blue.)*

But Commander Zaja about had a stroke when I said the word 'dye'... so I gave that idea up.

Puck is also very pale, but he's built differently or something. These Pathremiri women *(and men... and children...)* aren't freaked out by him, they're just sort of *baffled*. As if he reminds them of someone they knew a long time ago, but can't quite place.

And the kids sometimes come running up to him... so long as I'm not close by. I guess those would be the village pranksters.

I will say that *I* have no desire to play any pranks here.

If Selavan seemed too serious and full of itself... Pathremir seems *worse*.

I totally get why Amanita ran away.

This place is stultifying.

And I can see her trying not to let it smother her. There's a slightly desperate look in the back of her eyes each time after she has to play Princess of the Realm, and I seriously believe she would light off on her own if she had the chance. And that's despite how much she clearly wants to see her parents again.

I hope that's not what she saw in *me* at home...
I don't *think* Aldyrwald was quite so smothering.
On the other hand, I wasn't allowed out of sight of the castle...

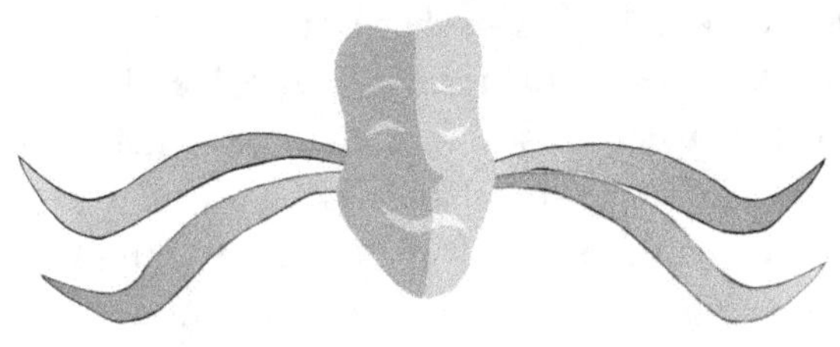

Day 79

We're arriving at the royal palace-city tomorrow.

We stopped early tonight so that everyone can freshen up and present a good face. Apparently, we are doing the Triumphal Entry of the Princess Returning from Her Tour of the World and everyone is going to pretend Amanita's departure was entirely planned.

She's pretty fidgety. She wanted to press on and see her parents *tonight,* and I can't blame her. I'd've felt the same way.

(Gods. Are Mama and Papa going to insist on doing this sort of thing when I go home eventually? I just want to jump off my steed – not Twinklestar by then, I assume, since I'll be married – and go hug them. Not that Aldyrwald does a lot of ceremonial-type stuff. We just aren't this **big.***)*

Daffyd looks... a great deal less enthusiastic. But then, he hasn't been gone nearly as long and he's not going back to be everyone's favorite. He was already pretty squished even when I first met him; now I can see how much more relaxed and freer he was out there on the Central Plains. Or even in Selavan.

It's as disheartening to see him stuffing himself into a smaller and smaller box with every day that passes as it is to see Amanita looking trapped by everybody's expectations that she act *regal* and *commanding. (Not that she doesn't do those things very effectively anyways.)*

Not that I can really help either of them.

Though I kind of think that if that Silver Dragon Goddess of theirs was willing to go to so much trouble to get Lochea to become Queen of Selavan to fix the troubles of women in *that* country... maybe She could put a little effort into fixing things for guys *here*.

I'm not sure what she could do for Amanita, but that would do something for Daffyd.

Well, I suppose it's not for me to criticize. Joanna and Priscilla and Roger more or less seemed to imply that they wouldn't intervene, even if I had to get married to some old middleborn princess who was going to assassinate me and Papa. Or that they'd have let the neighbors invade Aldyrwald.

They said something about there being Rules that Gods have to follow, but...

...sorry, not buying it.

They have so much Power. Surely, They should be using it to fix *problems*.

It's called 'free-will,' bro.

Okay, *so* weird when I end up writing down Twinklestar's thoughts. And I still don't buy it. And since when are we 'bros' again?

Since Chillabiaen told me she thinks the colors are cute.

Mares before bros, then?

There is nothing – and I do mean *nothing* – like the feel of someone *shrugging* inside your *head*.

I don't really recommend it.

Ugh. I'm going to bed. Tomorrow is going to be a *super* long day.

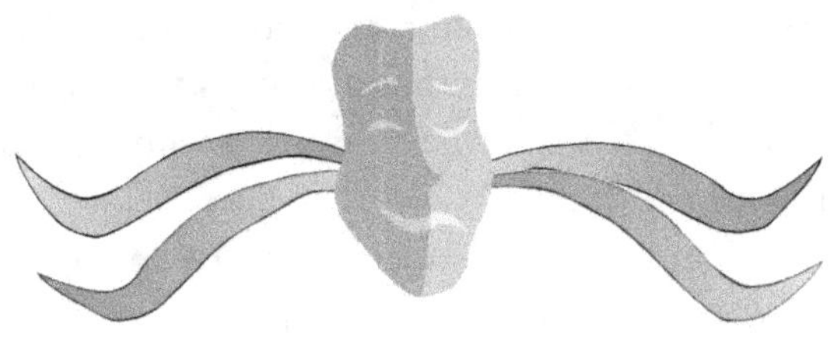

Day 80

since we left Flowerdust – like 112 or something since I left home

Yeah, it was a loooong day.

The Pathremiri capitol city is really big and spread out. *(I don't know if it even has a proper name – they just keep calling it the 'capitol city' or the 'palace-city' or even the 'Queen's city'.)*

There's very few buildings more than two stories tall, and most of them are only one level, so they keep having to build farther and farther out from the center, I guess. There were a few three-story buildings in clusters that Amanita said were marketplaces, so I guess those have to do with trade.

The palace itself is set off from everywhere else – there's a natural area preserved for royal use behind it, so no one can build there. And another side is taken up with parade grounds and training areas for the army.

I couldn't *see* any of that, of course, since everywhere is so incredibly *flat*.

The main body of the palace is about three stories, and it seems to be open on all sides, with these pillars and open breezy ways.

It seemed really weird to me, given the history of their invasion.

But I guess that *was* thousands of years ago.

Amanita says they use the mountains as their fortress now and if any enemy made it this far, the country would be lost anyways, so why not make it beautiful?

So, I asked about Winter storms and she made a face and said that a lot of it gets boarded up in the Winter.

So, it seems to be an aesthetic/philosophical thing. They're making a point – though to whom, I'm not sure, since it sounds like they discourage visitors from other lands other than trade caravans. And the trade caravans – we saw a few of them – are supposed to largely keep to themselves as they pass through, other than what they need to manage for business.

As he said he would, Puck and Chillabiaen disappeared shortly before we entered the city. I'm bummed, but Daffyd is *really* disappointed. Not sure why.

A larger troop of women warriors arrived this morning before we left the inn. They provided a Proper Escort for Her Royal Highness. Zaja was still in charge, however.

They set up the riding order with Zaja in front and a flagbearer beside her. Amanita followed right behind on Silverfoot, then Daffyd and I behind and to her flanks. The rest of the troop – and the new girls – formed up in a double column behind us. A couple were sent on ahead to clear the streets and announce our arrival.

With *trumpets,* for goodness' sake.

Personally, I thought it was a bit over the top.

Amanita straightened up to the most perfect posture I've ever seen on her and actually managed to look pretty regal.

There were people *(mostly women and girls, but some guys in the background)* actually *lining the streets.* And *cheering.*

Some of the children even had these little hand-sized flags with the same sigil as on the flag that our flagbearer *(ok,* **Amanita's** *flagbearer)* was waving out ahead of us: a sword, azure, crossed with a lightning-bolt, argent, over the stylized outline of mountains in argent, all of it on a ground of a dark, rather threatening, brownish-grey.

This was *definitely* over the top.

We rode through the city streets for awhile before coming to the palace. There was a wide courtyard or marketplace or... some sort of paved area surrounding the palace in all directions that I could see.

It was broken up with little gardens and fountains and stuff, but it definitely provided a good wide area – maybe twenty yards – that it would be next to impossible to get across without being spotted. And while the guard-towers are pretty discreet, I'm pretty sure I can see where they are.

If this is where Amanita ran away from, I'm impressed.

There were these wide, low stairs made of some kind of white stone on either side of a grand entrance. And a small group of people standing in the center of the entrance with women guards on either side.

We had to get off of our horses *(and Twinklestar – who is now back to his usual shade of glisteny white)* at the beginning of the open space and approach the royal party on foot.

The *other* royal party.

Though I suppose they were *more* royal, given that they included a ruling Queen.

Amanita's grandmother does *not* look like she's old enough to have grandchildren at all, let alone ones as old as Daffyd and Amanita. She barely looks older than Mama. And she's very lovely in the Pathremiri way – short and dark, with long black hair that either she dyes or it hasn't started to go grey. *(She was also wearing a very elegant gown. So were the other ladies with her. Guess Amanita's getting stuck wearing more dresses.)*

She came forwards and greeted both her grandchildren. It was kind of nice to see that she seemed nearly as pleased to see Daffyd as Amanita, given all that I'd heard and how Commander Zaja and her troupe treated him.

And then the Queen called their parents forwards to see them before anything else, which was thoughtful, as you could just see them itching to come forwards. Amanita's dad was clearly holding her mom so that she wouldn't break protocol. *(And he kept giving this **other** woman standing there these annoyed/anxious looks... and **that** woman kept glowering around at everyone... more about her in a minute.)*

Amanita's mom... doesn't look *anything* like her. *Or* anything like her own mother, the queen. She's taller and willowy and paler and *blonde. (Sort of blonde anyways, by comparison to everyone else around here. Anywhere else her hair would look like a rather light brown.)*

Amanita's dad looks more like a regular Pathremiri man – like Daffyd, but older.

Amanita seemed pretty happy to get hugs from her parents... and so did Daffyd, who's been gone nearly a year looking for her, as I understand it. It was nice to see there weren't recriminations – at least not in public – just honest relief that their children were home, safe.

Well, except for the sour expression on the other woman.

I really missed Mama and Papa right then. I hope they're as forgiving when I get home... eventually.

But then Commander Zaja was introducing me – and Twinklestar – to Queen Namarina, and I had to focus on greeting her properly. For a woman who spent most of our journey together acting as if she wished she'd never seen me, it was sort of remarkable how Zaja was now able to present me to her queen as if I was some prize she'd found all on her own.

And – for once – Twinklestar got a good amount of attention.

They had some serious appreciation for him in Selavan, where there's supposed to be some sort of unicorns-and-maidens community (*not that **we** got to check it out*), but he was still treated like... well, like a horse. Here he was treated like the intelligent being he is, and the queen greeted him as cordially as she did me.

She even politely invited him to join us inside the palace, but he just as politely declined (*through me*) and asked for a 'room' that lets out into a garden or pasture. And then he took charge of the rest of the horses and led them all off in the wake of a bowing stablemaster who was acting more like a horse's-butler.

And, yeah, that sounds weird now that I wrote it out. But he *was*.

And that was pretty much the end of the public formalities.

We were allowed inside (*and their adoring crowds did not follow us*)... to watch as the sour-looking woman ripped into Amanita for running off.

Apparently, this is her *other* grandmother. The one she always shuddered or grimaced over when mentioning. 'Eldest-Princess Reyalla' I've heard them call her.

Daffyd tried to speak up a couple of times to defend his sister, and so did the Prince-Consort Naeel, their father. And since that's his own *mom*, and she's pretty scary, that seemed fairly brave of him, to try.

Eldest-Princess Reyalla withered them both into silence with a glare and went back to berating Amanita.

Whom, I have to say, was being more meek about the whole thing than I've ever seen her.

Her mother, Princess-Heir Ytheril, stayed out of it, watching her own mother more than her daughter. Her expression was set in a neutral position, but there was something furious behind it – assuming I could read her.

Princess Ytheril actually didn't *not* look like Amanita once I got a closer look at her; it's just that her coloring is all different and she's slender instead of slightly stocky. *(Which might just be that Amanita is ready for **her** growth spurt... I mean **I'm** hardly a one to criticize!)*

I watched the Queen, trying to figure out why she was allowing this to go on. I mean, this was inside the closed doors of the royal palace, but it was hardly private; we were still in the vestibule, not the royal family's apartments or anything. There were warrior-women and servants everywhere.

And Amanita might have been feigning meekness, but every time her nasty grandmother shot down her mother or her father or her brother, I could see her starting to seethe. It was obvious that the explosion was only a matter of time...

It wasn't fair for her reunion with her parents to be so marred by this unpleasant woman *(I can't really call her an **old** woman... she looks older than Queen Namarina, but not by a lot)*. I knew that I'd hate it if Great-Uncle Sir Eddie does something like this when I get home. *(Or Roger's parents, or the other neighbors... which actually doesn't seem all that far-fetched.)*

So, I decided to speak up.

"Her Highness hasn't been 'gallivanting about,' Your Grace," I interrupted the latest tirade, stepping up to stand by my best friend. "She's been learning about the world, making important connections, and doing great deeds."

Eldest-Princess Reyalla turned her withering gaze on me, but *I* don't really care what she thinks of me, so I just gave her back look for look.

Which seemed to unnerve her a bit, presumably because Pathremiri guys *don't* stand up to women, but she rallied.

"Connections with *whom?*" she sneered. "We've had word about the political disaster *you* caused in Selavan, little boy. We finally sign papers to begin negotiations for a peace between our countries and *you* and *she* manage to mess it up. And this after we almost went to war because of her running away through Selavan three years ago!"

I could see Amanita's shoulders hunching a bit. This was one of the things that she actually feels guilty about, and I think the Eldest-Princess knew that somehow.

So, I put a hand on Amanita's shoulder and squeezed a little.

"Your *granddaughter* should be *honored* for being *brave* enough to explore other worlds. And *wise* enough to seek the aid of Iana warriors and unicorn-wise-women and the Fairy Queen Herself to do so. She should be *respected* for doing the hard work to stop a *war* that could have ripped all our worlds apart and helping to end both an Evil Wizard's and a rogue Dark-elf princess's reign of terror on the Central Plains. And helping to free some ten *thousand* people from their vile enchantments."

Amanita looked at me – looked *up* at me, because it looks like I really have grown a bit these last few months – and smiled.

Her parents looked impressed and pleased.

Apparently, I'm getting pretty good at these little impromptu speeches. I still don't know what an 'Iana warrior' is, but Amanita has made a big deal of traveling and training with one – several times – so I threw that in, too. After all, it doesn't matter if *I* know what that means so long as other people do.

"But you don't deny the political mess you created at Queen Lochea's Court?" Eldest-Princess Reyalla jumped on that omission as the Queen gave me a thoughtful look.

I lifted my chin. *(My still-hairless chin, dammit, and given that all the adult men here are bearded that means they'll probably see **me** as a little boy. Though Daffyd shaves...)*

"It was a harmless prank, Your Grace," I said, rather pointedly using her appellation, since she'd 'forgotten' to use mine. "No one got hurt, and I took full responsibility."

"A *prank.*" She looked at the Queen. "Just like this miscreant of a granddaughter of ours. I told you before, Namarina. Spoiling the girl and letting her get away with her nonsense would have bad results. And here they are. First, she runs away, putting the entire Realm at risk since neither you nor Ytheril could be bothered to have more than one daughter. And now she brings back a prankster 'prince.' I suppose you'll let her get away with marrying him and turning the whole *country* into a farce."

Wait, *what?*

Amanita looked about as alarmed at that as I felt. "I'm not marrying Thony, Grandmother."

"Definitely not!" I agreed,

Everyone – except for the two of us and Daffyd – looked surprised. Even Commander Zaja, who was still hanging around. And Daffyd looked a bit insufferable.

Amanita faced her grandmothers. "Thony is *Crown Prince* of *Aldyrwald*. He can't stay *here* for the rest of his life."

I folded my arms and nodded sharply, keeping my glare on the obnoxious Eldest-Princess.

Princess Ytheril spoke up for almost the first time now. Her voice reminds me of someone... "Then why *did* you come back to Pathremir with our daughter, Your Highness?"

"Why did he *leave* his homeland might be a better question," the Eldest-Princess sniffed. "More of this irresponsible gallivanting around, *I* suspect."

Needless to say, she didn't believe my brief explanation of the Mountain-Region's politics.

But Queen Namarina and Amanita's parents all looked interested. And invited me to explain in more detail over dinner after we settled into our rooms.

So, that was what happened.

Like I hoped, I've got a suite of rooms to myself here in the palace... Well, sort of to myself. There's quite a herd of servants taking care of things. I assume that will settle down in a day or two. Guests always rile a castle up, as I know from home.

And now I have to get gussied up and go talk to everyone again.

This loooong day just won't end.

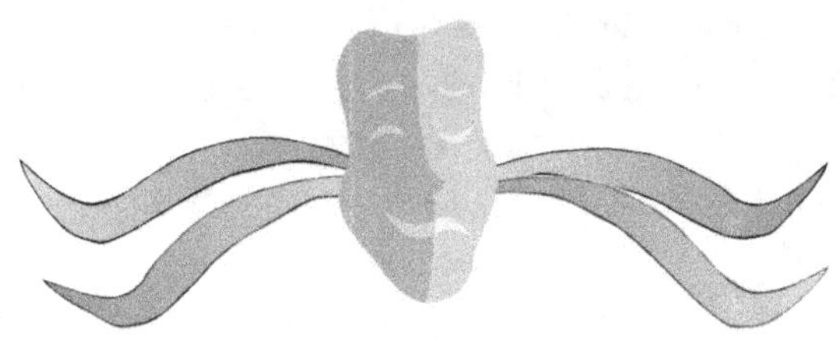

Day 81

since Flowerdust – technically, anyways

It's after midnight... like WAY after midnight, and I'm exhausted, but I can't sleep. And dang it, what's the good of having my own rooms if I can't get up and put on a lantern in the middle of the night if I feel like it?

So, I am.

Last night's dinner was just TOO CRAZY.

That's what's keeping me awake.

Well, that and wondering what in the name of 'all the worlds beyond the Fairy Wood' *(to quote someone or other)* I'm supposed to do *now*.

There are no available princesses in Pathremir. *(Well, her nasty grandmother suggested Amanita again, but um, NO.)*

There are a few 'fal-Princesses' – which is what they call their princesses who aren't in the line of succession – but they all seem to be married *(or something, there were some weird looks exchanged, but it didn't look like Amanita knew what that was all about)* and anyways they're all at *least* ten years older than me. And they're the sisters of Amanita's dad, which – even if that weren't *weird* – would make Eldest-Princess Reyalla my mother-in-law.

So, um, NO. Given the way she looks at me, the neighbors would have to stand in line to do me in.

And even if these women weren't *old* and *married (and **mothers** already)*, they don't really have command of any troops. Amanita looked a bit guilty over that, and her mom looked apologetic, but Queen Namarina was firm that she is not sending her people off to another world.

(I may have made an incautious remark about then, regarding the fact that the guys on my world wouldn't really take their women-warriors terribly seriously. I mean, I was trying to be practical and not disappointed, and make it clear I didn't harbor any grudges... but the Eldest-Princess glared at me, and the Queen looked displeased, Amanita rolled her eyes, and Prince Naeel looked amused.)

*(Daffyd told me later that there really **are** men in their armed forces. They're just not allowed to leave Pathremir. Or do ceremonial duty, like welcoming their prince and princess home... well, he just said 'princess.')*

There's a princess over in Dawil *(the next kingdom to the west)* who is reportedly very beautiful in a Prissy-kind of way. *(Prissy like my sister, Priscilla, but presumably without the bushy, black tail, not overly prim and proper.)*

She's nearly twenty, which I suppose isn't *too* bad. There's some weird complication about whether she's an only child or a youngest of two – but whichever way it is, she's not inheriting the throne, so that could be okay, I guess.

She's not a *middleborn,* anyways.

This Dawil-place is supposed to be pretty prosperous, so I guess I should check her out.

Twenty isn't *that* old, compared to fifteen, right?

Sigh.

I already know there aren't any princesses in Selavan or Dysacha *(or Brelsin or the other dinky places we traveled through... not that they had any real fighters to lend to my cause anyhow).* South is a country called Sethival – again, no princesses. And southeast is all that big, demon-filled plainsland that Daffyd told me about a while back.

So, if this dudette in Dawil doesn't work out... I guess I'm going to have to travel several *months* in some direction.

They keep talking about a university – maybe there are records of royal families. I should probably go there and check it out before heading off.

ANYways... back to the crazy dinner.

As I'd guessed, the Eldest-Princess didn't believe a word I had to say. She *hemmed* and *huffed* and *pooh-poohed* at everything I told them.

Which was *rude* as well as *annoying,* since I was just answering the Queen's questions.

I really don't understand what her deal is. Or how she fits into things. She acts like she has the right to order around not only her son, Prince-Consort Naeel *(and I thought the guys here got free of their moms when they got married),* but also Queen Namarina herself.

And the Queen doesn't quash her unless it gets so outrageously egregious that there's clearly no other option. Nor does the Eldest-Princess *stay* squished after a correction like that.

Although... she *was* pretty shocked at how the dinner ended... so, maybe...

Nah, I get the feeling nothing can stop that woman's mouth from running off and saying nasty stuff.

So, what happened was that we were re-hashing some of our adventures since leaving Aldyrwald *(I still haven't heard all of the story of how Amanita got there)* and the mess in Flowerdust. And Amanita and Daffyd and I were taking turns telling the story of how the whole thing went down at the end – you know, the way Kamauri fought Stillheart, and Raven'sWing suddenly died of old age, and the unicorns appeared, and one of them *(Quellarie)* turned human, and then Puck and Aleri arrived and Puck called in Lady Opalsinger and the Wild Hunt, and Stillheart rode off to try to get away from them, and then the Dark-elves and unicorns freed the zombies.

Well, Eldest-Princess Reyalla was *pooh-poohing* the whole thing, of course. When we got to the part about Puck being the God of Pranksters and it being the work of me and Amanita and Dae that had made him Powerful enough to break Stillheart's spell barricading the Fairy Wood... well, her lack of manners got the better of her again.

"*Who* did you say?" she scoffed. "A *God* of *Pranksters?*"

I tried not to grind my teeth. "His name is 'Puck,' Your Grace."

"*Who?*" she said again, affecting not being able to hear me... and the Queen had a very strange look on her face. And Daffyd – who, as I mentioned before, had gotten pretty close to Puck since leaving Selavan – was looking kind of mad.

"*Puck.*" I said, trying to keep my voice even, though I know it got a little higher as I got louder. *(And dang it, it's been* **months** *since I had trouble coping with unexpected pitch changes. It shouldn't have been a problem.)*

Reyalla made a dismissive, flipping gesture with her fingers. "If you can't speak sense, little boy, keep your lips sealed amongst your betters."

"He's a *Crown Prince,* Grandmother," Daffyd broke in. "That makes him the equivalent of *my* mother in rank and *your* superior."

His parents both winced and Amanita's eyes went wide. The Queen just sighed.

She looked down her nose at him – a good trick, since he's taller than her, even at the supper table. "No one asked *your* opinion. I'm not even sure why *you're* at this table at all. And you can't expect me to believe there's a God named *puke* or some such."

Daffyd looked absolutely furious.

"*That's PUCK, you horrid woman!*" he yelled.

Personally, I thought his reaction was a bit overdone.

And, technically, Puck is *my* God, I suppose. Or Amanita's. So, if anyone was going to get upset...

Later on, Daffyd told me it was just all the years of her abusing him and his parents and Amanita – he just *snapped* for a moment.

"Don't you *swear* at me, young man!" his mean grandmother yelled back.

No one seemed particularly surprised by this exchange, so I'm not sure I buy Daffyd's explanation. Personally, I think it had more to do with how close he's gotten with Puck over the last month or so. He seems... a bit less, ah, *restrained* here than he did while we were traveling. Is he maybe more scared of Commander Zaja than of the Eldest-Princess?

"Puck, Puck, Puck! That's the *name* of the Prankster God." Daffyd said hotly, "I'm not *swearing* at you, Grandmother."

And then suddenly...

...Puck *appeared.*

Standing in the middle of the table with a rather confused expression – and a fork in one hand and a small plate in the other. And some sort of red, blobby thing on his fork.

"Um, somebody called?" Puck asked. "Oh, hi, Daffyd."

By coincidence *(or incantation?)* he'd appeared facing Daffyd. Who was sitting between the Eldest-Princess *(at the foot of the table)* and his father.

Unsurprisingly, Reyalla looked offended... though in this case, I have to say she had some justification. Having a guy – in boots, no less, even if they're *elegant,* pale green, silver-trimmed boots and match the rest of his fancy dinner attire – suddenly appear on top of the dinner table is a bit... unsettling.

"Oh, um, hi..." Daffyd looked rather shocked himself. "I, uh, I didn't mean to call you away from anything..."

Puck shrugged nonchalantly and handed over the fork and dessert-dish to the Pathremiri prince before hopping off the table between him and the Eldest-Princess. "No big deal. Mother's deputies were insisting on having a super-boring reception to welcome me home. And I don't think I told you that saying my name three times would summon me."

His gaze swept over Eldest-Princess Reyalla without a great deal of interest before noticing me and Amanita, as he began to turn around. "Hi, Thony, Amanita. You're both dressed up tonight, aren't... you..."

Puck's words trailed off as he turned far enough to see the Queen.

And he stopped turning.

And *she* rose to her feet, eyes meeting his, and... she was trembling. *She* clearly knew who he was.

There was a long, awkward moment.

Daffyd tried to break into it by saying, "Um, as long as you're here, Puck, I want you to meet my parents and my grandmother... er, grand*mothers*..." He looked at Eldest-Princess Reyalla unhappily, but for once she didn't seem to notice.

Nor did Puck.

"Namarina," he said softly, "You're as beautiful as the last time I saw you."

"Skift..." she said with... too much feeling apparently, because this *serious, ruling Queen* gave a nervous little laugh and broke their gaze. "Flatterer. My mirror tells me every day that I'm not nineteen anymore."

That... didn't make a lot of sense to me, but I could see Daffyd and Amanita were exchanging significant looks. *(They aren't terribly good at being discreet when they do these things. They screw up their faces in all these weird expressions. It's more like they're arguing with their facial muscles than trying to sneak some information past the other people they're with. Very strange. Prissy and I learned to keep those sorts of things discreet before I was five.)*

Puck didn't look away from her, but skirted the table to go over to her. He gave Daffyd a quick squeeze of the shoulder before he did, paused to clap Prince Naeel on the back, and paused for a moment to look at Princess Ytheril.

Who... looks a good bit like him.

He smiled at her, then faced her mother. The Queen.

"Not a bit of flattery, Namarina. If anything, the years have made you *more* beautiful. You hardly look older than our daughter."

And when he opened his arms and the Queen stepped into them... well, *I* wasn't surprised by that point.

But apparently, I was the only one who wasn't.

Princess Ytheril and Eldest-Princess Reyalla and Amanita all started speaking at once, which meant none of it was making any sense. And the Queen and Puck – *Prince Skiftglow* – had gotten to the kissing parts, so they weren't even trying to make sense to anyone else.

Daffyd and I left at some point. *(After polishing off the remaining food, of course.)*

He was as stunned as everyone else – but there really wasn't any point in guys trying to get a word in edgewise right then and there. His dad stayed at the table, watching the commotion, but he waved us to go on. I guess he was sticking around to... support his wife? Or his daughter?

Or, um, meet his father-in-law?

Does it count if they weren't ever actually married?

That's when Daffyd explained about there being men in their army and how he yelled at his grandmother *(Eldest-Princess Reyalla)* because he just *snapped*. And claimed it had never happened before. *(Which, as I noted previously, I seriously doubt.)*

I had a million questions, but he looked sort of dazed and said he was going to bed and we can talk tomorrow.

Which I guess makes sense. I mean, it's not every day you find out your good friend is your grandfather. Or that your grandfather is a *God*.

I took it in stride, I think, but I've sort of been through this before. From a different perspective, and Joanna and Priscilla being Goddesses doesn't make *me* part-divine or anything, so I suppose it's not the same thing.

But yeah, Puck is Princess Ytheril's dad. And she didn't know. *No one* knew.

I guess that's why Amanita is such a great prankster. *(My own gifts in that direction are clearly not inherited.)*

And now that I've written all this stuff down, I think I'm going to sleep.

This was a crazy, long journey and it looks like the crazy isn't stopping now.

Maybe I can get away from it all and check out that university place.

Or maybe I'll just enjoy living in luxury again for awhile first.

I'll figure it out...... *(that was a yawn, and my pencil dragged on the paper)*

I'll figure it out tomorrow.

Or something.

MAP that Daffyd shows Thony

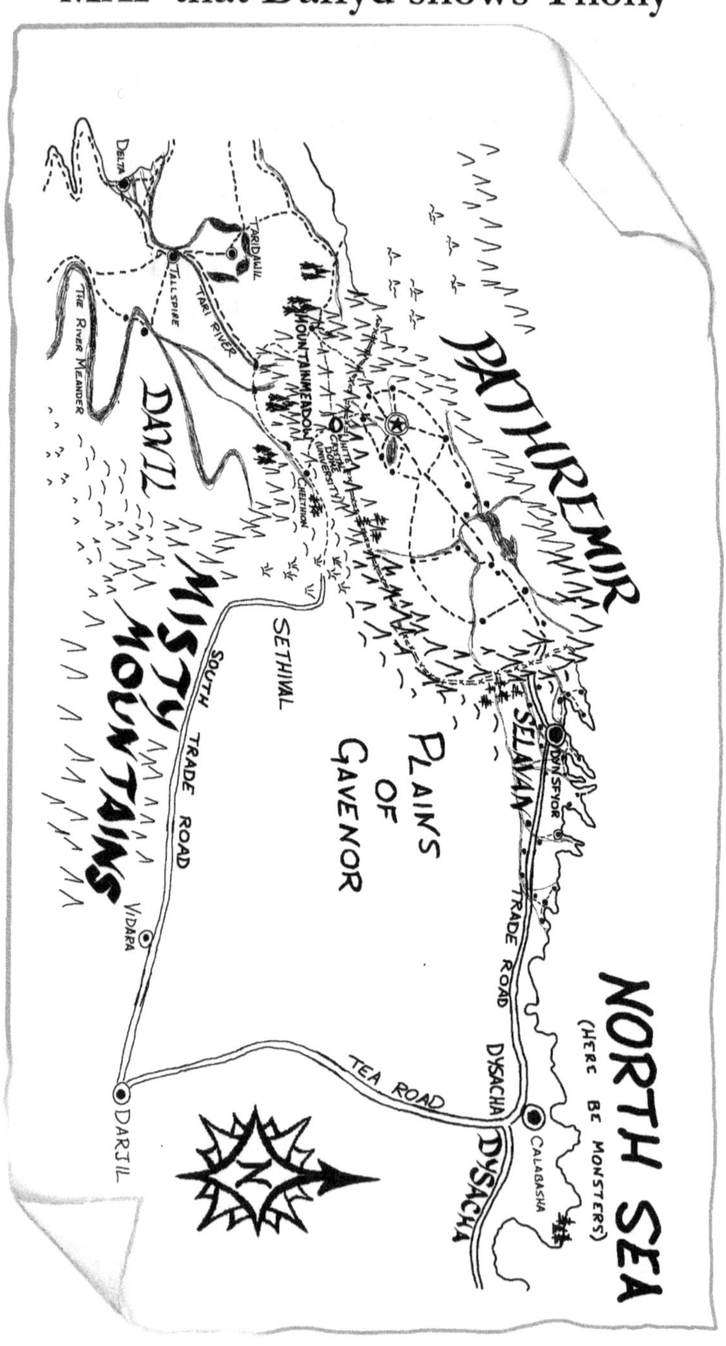

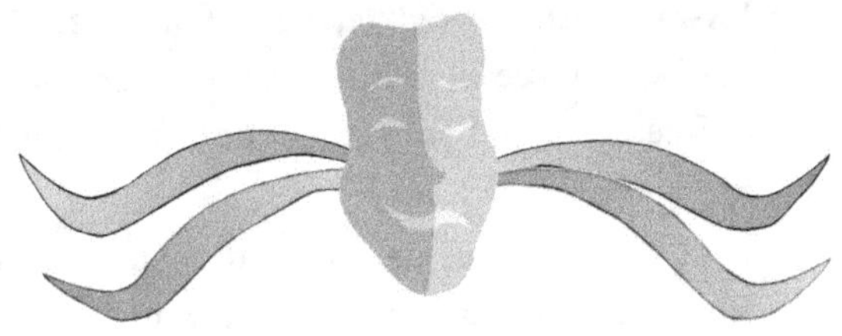

Index of Characters

- People who are along on the Journey from Flowerdust:
    - o Amanita (a.k.a. 'Nita, a.k.a. the Lost Princess of Pathremir). Thony's friend and co-prankster. Younger sister of Daffyd.
    - o Daffyd. Prince of Pathremir. Amanita's older brother.
    - o Puck. (a.k.a., Prince Skiftglow). The 'King of Pranksters', a fairy attendant of Queen Lilysong. Son of Queen Snowmistral of the Snow-Fairies.
    - o Silverfoot. Thony's rather-too-energetic horse.
    - o Thony (Prince Anthony Devinthal the Affable and the Affirmative). Crown Prince of Aldyrwald. Younger brother of Princess Joanna and Princess Priscilla. Unicorn-maiden Bound to Twinklestar.
    - o Twinklestar. Unicorn, Bound to Thony, friend of Amanita.
    - o Zaja, Commander. A warrior woman from Pathremir.

- People in Dysacha
    - o Videl, King of Dysacha. Father of Evelynne.
    - o Evelynne, Crown Princess of Dysacha. King Videl's daughter

- People in Selavan
    - o Heidelkill, Dowager Duchess of. An elderly woman who apparently uses laundry soap to wash her hair.
    - o Inga Einirsgeld. Daughter (youngest child) of Count and Countess Einirsgeld. Granddaughter of Lady Wisdom. Apprentice sorceress and bibliophile. "Manager" of Dauntless Books.

o Jessina Keetering (a.k.a. Jess). Oldest of Davril's younger sisters. Fiancée of Lord Torsthyn Danessen. An employee of Keetering-and-Salwan Banking and Fiduciary Institution Private Limited.

o Kyrista Keetering. Davril's youngest sister. An employee of Keetering-and-Salwan Banking and Fiduciary Institution Private Limited.

o Lochea, Disciple of the Goddess of Light and Darkness, co-Disciple of the Lord of Light with King Mithral. Luminous Queen of Selavan and wife of King Mithral.

o Madame Graciella Keetering. Mother of Davril, Jessina, Mikeira, Kyrista. Wife of Mister Geyorg Keetering. An employee and Board member of Keetering-and-Salwan Banking and Fiduciary Institution Private Limited.

o Mister Geyorg Keetering. Father of Davril, Jessina, Mikeira, Kyrista. Husband of Madame Graciella Keetering. President of Keetering-and-Salwan Banking and Fiduciary Institution Private Limited.

o Mithral. King of Selavan, Disciple of the Lord of Light. Effulgent King Husband of Queen Lochea.

o Torsthyn Danessen. Young nobleman engaged to Jessina Keetering.

o Wisdom, Lady. Common-use title of the Dowager-Countess Einirsgeld. Premier sorceress of Selavan. Grandmother of Inga. Owner of Dauntless Books.

• People in Pathremir

o Naeel, Prince-Consort. Amanita and Daffyd's dad. Husband of Princess-Heir Ytheril, son of Eldest-Princess Reyalla.

o Namarina, Queen. Queen of Pathremir, Amanita's maternal grandmother.

o Reyalla, Eldest-Princess. Amanita's paternal grandmother.

o Ytheril, Princess. Princess-Heir of Pathremir, daughter of Queen Namarina, Amanita and Daffyd's mother, wife of Prince Naeel.

- People who were in Flowerdust
    - o Aleri. Demi-God of Healing, Lies, Rogues… and Politics. Son of the Goddess Sifwisa of the Trade-Winds.
    - o Aspenheart, Lord. Prince of the Light-elves, an attendant of the Fairy Queen.
    - o Dae Goldeneyes. Youngest mercenary ever. A graduate of Sonoro's School of Soldiering.
    - o Daennor Cat'sFoot. Mercenary. Partner of Kamauri Spiralspear. A graduate of Sonoro's School of Soldiering.
    - o Daphne. Istevan and Davril's baby daughter. (Biological parents: Julanna Silversea and Valderon Raven'sWing.)
    - o Davril (a.k.a., Dav). Daphne's father, Istevan's husband. A cousin of Julanna Silversea. Older brother of Jessina, Mikeira, and Kyrista Keetering, son of Mister Geyorg and Madame Graciella Keetering. Heir to the Keetering-and-Salwan Banking and Fiduciary Institution Private Limited.
    - o Evrien Quickfoot. A very old mercenary. Temporary Guildhouse-Keeper in Flowerdust. A graduate of Arazia's Academy at Arms.
    - o Istevan Highblade (called Slyblade, a.k.a Stev). Davril's husband, Daphne's father. A mercenary spy who worked with Julanna Silversea. A graduate of Sonoro's School of Soldiering.
    - o Jost. Leader of a gang of street-kids in Flowerdust, now Davril's apprentice banker.
    - o Julanna Silversea. A Bard spying on Valderon Raven'sWing's forces in Flowerdust. Biological mother of Daphne. Former girlfriend to Valderon Raven'sWing
    - o Kamauri Spiralspear. Mercenary and unicorn-maiden. Bound to Rainsparkle, partner with Daennor Cat'sFoot. Friend of Dae Goldeneyes. A graduate of Sonoro's School of Soldiering.
    - o Opalsinger, Lady. Princess of the Dark-elves, attendant of the Fairy Queen.
    - o Quellarie Unicorn-Born. Wise-woman/unicorn.
    - o Rainsparkle. Unicorn. Bound to Kamauri Spiralspear.

- o Shalladra Stillheart (called 'Icicleblood'). Valderon Raven'sWing's co-conspirator and a Dark-elf. Aunt of Princess Opalsinger.

- o Valderon Raven'sWing (deceased). An Evil Wizard who wanted to take over the world (or possibly all the worlds) along with Shalladra Stillheart. Former boyfriend of Julanna Silversea.

- **Some Fairly Cool People Back on Thony's homeworld:**
  - o Annabel (Queen Annabel of Aldyrwald). Wife of King Bill; mother of Joanna, Priscilla, and Thony.
  - o Bill (King Bill / King William Devinthal of Aldyrwald). Husband of Queen Annabel. Father of Joanna, Priscilla, and Thony.
  - o Cythera, the New Goddess of Fire
  - o Jeremy. Centaur, husband of Priscilla.
  - o Joanna (Princess Joanna Devinthal the Wise and Wonderful). Eldest-born princess of Aldyrwald. Daughter of King Bill and Queen Annabel; sister of Priscilla and Thony. Wife of Prince Sir Roger. The New Goddess of the Earth.
  - o Priscilla (Princess Priscilla Devinthal the Bright-Eyed and Bushy-Tailed, aka Prissy). Second-born princess of Aldyrwald. Daughter of King Bill and Queen Annabel; sister of Joanna and Thony. Wife of Jeremy. The New Goddess of Animals (including humans) and of Love/ Fertility.
  - o Raymond (Crown Prince of Schwannsberg). Roger's older brother. Oldest son of King Richie and Queen Janet.
  - o Richie (King of Schwannsberg). Roger and Raymond's father. Husband of Queen Janet. Former best friend of King Bill.
  - o Roger (Prince of Schwannsberg and Knight). Second-born son of King Richie and Queen Janet. Husband of Joanna. The New God of Air.
  - o Wes. Amanita and Thony's friend, a stableboy.

- People Who are Elsewhere (or Elsewhen), but are Still Important Anyways:
    - o Goddess of Light and Darkness. Goddess of Selavan and Pathremir. The Silver Dragon.
    - o Fairy Queen, The… also the Great Goddess Who Guards the Ways Between the Worlds (a.k.a., the Waywalker).
    - o Karia. Seeress of the Líonar who led them to Cross the Worlds and come to Pathremir.
    - o Lord of Light. God of Selavan.
    - o Midele Featherspray. A novice priestess of the Golden Sphinx on Eyola, Girona's cousin.
    - o Mikeira Keetering (a.k.a., Miki). Davril's middle sister.
    - o Silver Dragon. See Goddess of Light and Darkness.
    - o Snowmistral, Queen of the Snow-Fairies (a.k.a. Sylphara of the Mountain-Breezes, Goddess of Blizzards and Gales). Mother of Puck/Skiftglow. Patron Goddess of Pathremir and Mountainmeadow.
    - o Sylphara. See Snowmistral.
    - o Varella (deceased). Historical First Queen of Pathremir. She overthrew the Líonar ruling class (including her husband) and founded the Pathremiri Line of Queens.

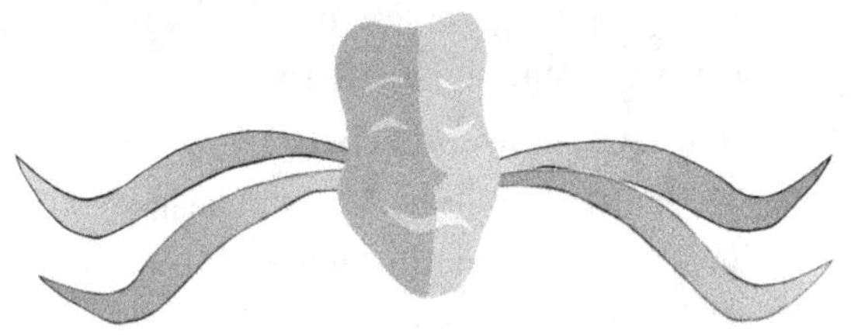

Index of Places

- On Thony's homeworld:
    - o Aldyrwald. The country where Thony is Crown Prince. Three linked valleys, centrally located in the mountain region.
    - o Schwannsberg. A neighboring country, and the one Thony's brother-in-law Roger hails from. Presumably they are the one neighbor not interested in invading Aldyrwald.

- Other worlds:
    - o Eyola. The world that Midele and Girona are from.
    - o Fairy Wood. Ruled by Queen Lilysong. A forest that bridges the gap between many worlds. Only the fairies and elves know how to navigate it by nature, though others can learn.

- Amanita's homeworld:
    - o Brelsin. A country in the plains that regularly gets overrun by invaders. On Amanita's homeworld. East of Pathremir, Sethival, Selavan, Plains of Gavenor, Dawil, the Merutian Sea.
    - o Central Plains. The wide, grassy area that contains Brelsin and a number of other city-states that are perpetually at odds.
    - o Darjil. A town about ten days' ride from Flowerdust. They grow the best tea. Also, their entire population was enchanted by Valderon Raven'sWing.
    - o Dawil. A prosperous country very far to the west of Flowerdust.

o Dynsfyor. Largest city on the North Coast. Capitol of Selavan. Home of Davril and Istevan.

o Dysacha. The country between the northernmost point of the Tea Road and the North Coast.

o Flowerdust. A small nowhere-sort of town in Brelsin that ended up as Raven'sWing's base for invading the Fairy Wood. It's where Thony and the rest defeated Raven'sWing and Stillheart.

o Misty Mountains. The mountain-range where Pathremir is located.

o Muana Desert. A vast desert located to the south of the Central Plains.

o North Coast. The North Coast of the continent that Flowerdust, Dysacha, Selavan, and Pathremir are located on.

o Pathremir. A country in the Misty Mountains. Amanita's homeland.

o Plains of Gavenor. A demon-haunted area west of Brelsin.

o Selavan. A country ruled by King Mithral and Queen Lochea. West of Brelsin, adjacent to Pathremir and the Plains of Gavenor. Includes a famous school for Bards and an enclave for unicorn-maidens.

o Tea Road. The road that runs from Darjil in the south to Dysacha in the north. It also makes a T with the Coastal Road.

o Sonoro's School of Soldiering. Famous school for mercenaries. Graduates include the current headmistress, Taridanae Foxheart, Istevan Highblade, Kamauri Spiralspear, Daennor Cat'sFoot, and Dae Goldeneyes.

o University of the White Crystal Dome. An institution of higher learning located between Pathremir and Dawil in the Misty Mountains.

THONY
and the Much-Anticipated Adventure

Book One
of the
Prankster Prince

MANGALA MCNAMARA

132

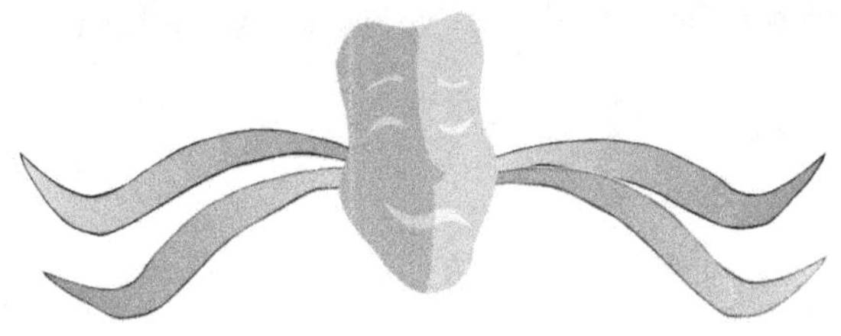

Chapter ONE
A Princely Punch

Crown Prince Anthony Devinthal the Affable (and the Affirmative) of the valley-kingdom of Aldyrwald – an inconsequential kingdom on a substandard continent on an unimportant world –slouched along a corridor of his father's castle, kicking a small rock that someone *(probably him)* had tracked into the castle earlier.

It wasn't *fair.*

His parents were ridiculously overprotective – all because Thony was Heir to the Throne. Queen Annabel had vapors when Thony went out of sight of the castle, even into the *very safe and well-maintained* woods beyond the village. King Bill started to *harumph* and look pale when Thony casually suggested a visit to the next valley-kingdom over, the one ruled by King Bill's best friend who also happened to be the father-in-law of Thony's older sister, Joanna – even *without* Thony hinting that a detour to check out the local giant along the way might be interesting.

Being a crown prince was *seriously boring.*

And anytime he tried to do something to *make* things a little less boring he ended up in trouble.

Today being a case in point.

It was his mother's fault really. She knew better than to come into his rooms.

For goodness' sake, the *servants* knew better than to come into his rooms.

Thony hadn't even been *in* there when Mama had opened the door, taken one look, screamed, and fainted.

Someone had been sensible enough to summon Joanna.

Someone *else* had tracked down Thony and seen him into the throneroom to face his father for a little chat about what King Bill called his 'misdemeanor'. *("<u>You're</u> the one who's meaner!" Thony had yelled in what was, perhaps, <u>not</u> the best display of behavior for a young man who was a few months away from fifteen. No matter that his parents seemed intent on treating him like he was <u>five</u>.)*

So now he was stuck with a fortnight of double-length protocol lessons with Master Eswith – the excruciatingly boring teacher who had reportedly convinced the eternally patient and polite Joanna to threaten to run away from home. *(That was the rumor anyways, passed on from Thony's middle sister, Priscilla. Joanna had been out from under Master Eswith's gentle care years before either of them had begun, though, so how Prissy knew this bit of intelligence was somewhat questionable.)*

An hour with Master Eswith was bad enough and what Thony had to suffer through on a regular basis. By two hours, the young prince was usually falling asleep and the 'gentle master' was beating him about the head and hands with a wooden ruler to *prove* that Thony had fallen asleep and Thony was plotting vengeance on Eswith and whichever parent had stuck him in double-length lessons. The one time King Bill had sentenced him to *three*-hour long lessons, Thony had plotted vengeance on the entire castle.

No one had ever considered doing that again, even though it had been almost five years and he'd grown a bit more of a sense of proportion. Apparently, the memory of caterpillars everywhere – in the bedsheets, in shoes, in the cabinets of clean dishes *(but not in the <u>food</u>. He wasn't an idiot after all)* – still lingered.

Thony kind of agreed that he'd deserved what he'd gotten for that one – helping clean up all the mess – but most of his pranks were much more amusing and innocuous. And he still got in trouble with his father over them. *(And <u>honestly</u>? How seriously could you take a man who let his subjects call him 'King Bill'? Thony had long ago decided that if anyone tried to call him 'King Thony' when <u>he</u> was crowned, he'd lop their heads off. Except his sisters. And their husbands; Roger and Jeremy were cool. And <u>maybe</u> his mother.)*

Princes were supposed to go on adventures and do interesting things. Instead, his *sisters* had gone off on The Quest a year earlier – and Left Him Behind. Instead, he'd been stuck *here* in *the most boring place in the Entire Universe.* And with no real hope that he would *ever* get to go *anywhere* or do *anything* interesting. *Ever.*

Of course, he didn't really blame his sisters *(or Prince Roger, the second-born prince from the neighboring kingdom)* for going on The Quest. They'd kind of had to, after the debacle that Prissy's sixteenth birthday party had become. But they'd left him behind.

They'd come back a few months later. Both of his sisters had gotten married while they were gone, though Mama and Papa had insisted that Joanna and Roger, at least, go through a second wedding ceremony *('for propriety's sake' – as if the very fact of Priscilla and Joanna secretly going off on The Quest hadn't taken everything so far beyond the pale of 'propriety' that there was no real way back. But the wedding had made Mama and Papa happier, not to mention King Richie and Queen Janet. Though Roger's older – and as yet unmarried – brother, Raymond, had kept giving both of the newlyweds odd looks as if he <u>wanted</u> to be happy for them, but couldn't quite stop wondering if they were planning to usurp the throne he was to inherit someday.)*

But Joanna had married *Roger*, whom they'd known forever. Mama and Papa were more or less refusing to acknowledge Priscilla's husband at all.

His sisters *(and Roger)* had also come back with the news that their magick-poor world was about to undergo a 'Ragnarök'. All the Gods they had been worshiping forever were about to *die* and be replaced by new ones. And the new ones just *happened* to be: Joanna and Roger and Priscilla – and the handful of friends they had brought back from The Quest.

Oh, and after all that, magick would be much more available to use. For everyone, not just the wisewomen and hermits and witches and sorcerers.

135

Mama and Papa's skepticism had been palpable. *(No one else than them and Thony had been told about the creation of new Gods at the time, although the word of the 'Ragnarök' had been duly passed along – no doubt with the tale growing less believable with every iteration.)* Princesses falling asleep for a hundred years and princes turning into swans and evil witches and ogres and such were par for the course in their opinion, but *Gods?*

And Joanna and Roger and Priscilla weren't even lucky-numbered children. Joanna was at least an eldest child, but she'd had the bad taste to then have a pair of younger siblings – nine years later, though apparently it hadn't been for lack of effort on King Bill and Queen Annabel's parts at attempting to properly produce three children *(of one gender)* or seven or twelve. *(Or even <u>thirteen</u>, though that number usually created more problems than it solved. King Bill was the oldest of seven brothers, and Queen Annabel was the youngest of seven sisters with three older brothers as well.)*

But Roger and Priscilla were both second-borns.

And then there was Prissy's tail.

Supposedly she'd been born the absolute epitome of perfect princesshood – golden-haired, bright blue eyes *(they were really more green, but for marketing purposes were blue)*, fair skin, the works. But somewhere in the handful of minutes between her birth and being Presented to the Populace, Priscilla had acquired a bushy, black tail that was nearly as long as she was.

When the tail had fallen out of her baby blankets during her Presentation to the Populace – and it was obviously attached to the baby – their father, King Bill, had fainted. *(Which wasn't a <u>manly</u> thing to do, but what can you do when the guy tells people to call him 'King Bill'?)*

Unfortunately, he'd been holding the baby.

Fortunately – despite all the adults frozen in horror around her – nine-year-old Princess Joanna was the only person who had the presence of mind to dash forwards and rescue her baby sister from their falling father. And then to stand up before all the people *(who had been seriously confused, I mean, <u>nothing</u> interesting ever happened here)* and declaim that it was a fine tail. That, in fact it was quite likely the finest tail a princess had ever had. And then she told everyone to call Prissy 'Princess Priscilla the Bright-Eyed and

136

Bushy-Tailed' *(which might be where all these ridiculous appellations attached to the royal children had gotten started, though at least Joanna had gotten 'the Wise and Wonderful'. Not that Thony begrudged his sisters theirs, but 'the Affable and the Affirmative'? Yeesh!)* and the poor, confused crowds had cheered enthusiastically.

That was all fine with the Local Populace and even their own minor nobility were willing to go along with things, but Word had gotten out *(Mama said Word always did)* and the royalty in all the neighboring kingdoms had decided the Devinthals had Bad Blood and decided to avoid them. Except for Roger's parents, of course, since King Richie and King Bill had been friends since they were boys.

But since the local nobility of a given valley tended to follow the lead of their king, it meant that all of King Bill's pages and squires were the scions of local families, and all of Queen Annabel's ladies-in-waiting were as well. This was potentially something of a problem, since the girls and boys were sent up to the castle to find a spouse as much as to learn some useful skills, but King Richie had traded them a couple *(which was how they'd gotten to know Roger so well in the first place, though it seemed likely he hadn't been granted permission from King Richie to ask for Joanna's hand – so perhaps even best-friendship only went so far in the matter of Bad Blood)* and if there were somewhat fewer of each group than the king and queen would like, because some of their own more remotely located nobility had sent *their* scions off to other kingdoms, it didn't bother *Thony* at all.

He was busy mulling over all this old history and the Utter Unfairness of having been Left Behind while his sisters had Adventures in the Fairy Wood and how his small attempts to liven up this deadly boring place were met with such an extreme underappreciation... So he wasn't really paying attention to where that rock was going and he nearly tripped over the girl scrubbing the floor.

Well.

Actually, his rock skittered into her bucket and knocked it over, even though he hadn't kicked it all *that* hard.

And *then* this midget-sized girl popped up practically under his chin and belted him a solid one in the gut.

And *then*, while he was stumbling away in surprise, he slipped in the soapy water and fell down, landing on top of the angry girl.

Who called him clumsy and overweight *(which he wasn't, thank you very much, either one. He'd been lanky until a couple years ago and now was sort of... stocky. Priscilla said he was just getting ready for a growth spurt, and she should know if anyone did, since she was now the Goddess of Animals – which apparently included humans, to Mama and Papa's even greater dismay).*

She also called him a thoughtless oaf... and that one struck a bit closer to home, given that he knew that a prince should always be considerate of his People and he really *should* have been more aware of where that rock was going. But he hadn't, because he hadn't been paying attention. Which was sort of the whole problem in a nutshell.

And anyways the whole thing was just too embarrassing. Getting beaten up by a teeny little girl who looked like she was maybe ten – and him almost fifteen? That dinky thing had a right hook that out-sized her for sure! And if he should have to try to explain this to someone...

No. Nope. *Not* happening.

Thony had sloshed halfway down the corridor and almost around the corner when he realized there was something in his *pants*. Something that was *cold* and *wriggling* – and in his *under*pants, or it would have fallen out down his pantleg since Thony didn't hold with hose or tight pants.

It turned out to be a frog and it was alive and relatively unsquished when he got it out... which was a relief, though what he'd had to do to *get* it out in good order had been somewhat embarrassing.

That was when he heard the laughter.

He turned around and saw the scrubbing girl, hands on her hips, and laughing her head off at his antics.

Thony's first reaction was to scowl resentfully at her, but after a scant moment his expression changed to a sheepish grin. He'd stuffed enough frogs down other people's clothes *(though never their* <u>underpants</u> *– and how had she managed to do that without him noticing?)* that he had a fair idea of what he must have looked like. And it *was* pretty funny.

"He's getting away! Help me catch him!" The girl splashed sudsy water as she darted after the frog that was merrily hopping away from them.

Thony followed her without a question. Frogs – as pretty much everyone from Mama to Joanna to Priscilla had informed him on more than one occasion – *didn't* belong in the castle. The stone floors were too hard and dry for a creature that spent much of its life submerged in water, and the servants did too good a job at cleaning even the remotest dusty corners so there weren't enough insects for it to eat. *(Though Mama's concerns were rather different than his or his sisters'.)*

And chasing a frog through the castle together was generally silly enough to make anyone either fast friends or mortal enemies.

Honestly, Thony didn't care which. Either one would lighten the incredible boringness of life in Aldyrwald.

Fortunately, they caught up with the frog just inches before it would have leapt into his mother's solarium to wreak havoc on ladies-in-waiting and embroidery hoops alike.

Not so fortunately, Mama came over to see the commotion at the door, spotted the frog, and fainted. Again.

Joanna was sent for and Thony and the girl were made to wait for her while the ladies-in-waiting waved smelling salts under Queen Annabel's nose and placed cold cloths on her head and gossiped in quiet, giggly voices.

"Twice in one *day*, Thony?" Even Joanna's ever-patient tone sounded exasperated. "What are you trying to do? Get Papa to keep you from ever seeing the light of day again? At this rate even Master Eswith will run out of protocol lessons."

"Um, no...?" She'd phrased it as a question, but Thony had the feeling it was rhetorical.

"And now you're involving the *servants* in your pranks again?" And *that* was disappointment, and if there was anyone whom Thony actually *cared* about not disappointing, it was Joanna.

"It wasn't a prank! The frog just sort of... escaped. And I knocked over her bucket. And then she helped catch it." Which was all true, if slightly out of order. And definitely gave the impression that the frog had been *his* to start, rather than that *he* had been the victim of the *girl's* prank.

There didn't seem to be any good way out of this one. Thony looked at his feet. The girl had the frog, so he couldn't even pretend he was looking at it.

Priscilla bustled up right then – presumably summoned by Joanna in that God-Way they had now, or else called by the frog in her role as Goddess of Animals. She plucked the frog out of the girl's hands and headed back out, cooing at it, and only noticing Thony by way of a quick ruffling of his red curls. She had that look she got when someone interrupted what Thony had nicknamed 'Jeremy-time' – though apparently part of being a Goddess was the ability to appear perfectly turned out in a proper, princessly pink and frilly daygown when one might be seen by one's mother and her ladies.

So much for his best friend since forever.

Jeremy was cool, of course – and how cool was it to have a *centaur* for a brother-in-law? – but Priscilla never had time for Thony anymore.

"The bucket got tipped over? I'd imagine that's how the frog escaped – and why the pair of you are dripping suds," Joanna said thoughtfully after Priscilla had disappeared.

Her eyes looked like she had rather more of an idea of what had happened than that... like she could just look into Thony's own *soul* and pull the truth right out of him. And maybe she really *could*, now that she was the Goddess of the Earth and all. Though she'd been giving him *that* kind of look pretty much ever since he'd first discovered frogs when he was two or three years old, so it might just be a Joanna-Thing and not a Goddess-Thing.

"I should probably get that water taken care of and finish cleaning the floor before anyone slips in it and gets hurt," the girl suggested. Thony decided he needed to remember that little crease between the brows that did such an excellent job of suggesting Concern and Responsibility. Not that it would likely do *him* much good, given that everyone in the castle tended to assume that if there was something crazy going on he was probably the cause of it.

To be fair, they were usually right.

And it was his honor and his privilege to liven things up a little.

Even if it did extend those interminable lessons with Master Eswith.

Joanna looked at him with a fair amount of empathy. "I'll tell you what, Thony, you go help this girl clean up all that soapy water and we'll just call it even. I'll make things right with Mama."

That was... not entirely unexpected. Joanna's approach to discipline was all about 'natural consequences', which translated into 'fixing what you'd messed up'. And since cleaning up the messes he'd helped create was *far and away* more interesting than protocol lessons, Thony far preferred it when *she* got to sort him out.

However, he did kind of have to admit that King Bill's approach was probably a more effective deterrent. Not only did it leave the energetic young prince less time to think up new ways to create havoc, but adding to the overall boringness of Aldyrwald – especially in his own personal life – went against every principle he tried to live by.

Though if he managed to stay *awake* while listening to Master Eswith droning on about what fork to use at dinner for which esoteric side-dish that would probably never show up on Thony's plate, he often could daydream up some of his best ideas. Unfortunately, Master Eswith dealt with daydreaming about the same as he did actual sleeping, and bruises from that ruler could really hurt.

"Thanks, Joanna, you're the best!" He stretched up and gave her a kiss on the cheek, then trotted after the girl. She'd taken Joanna's comment as a permission to leave and had almost disappeared around a corner already. He had to move fast to catch up.

Find out what happens next in

Thony and the Much-Anticipated Adventure

Available in eBook, paperback and hardcover at all fine online bookstores!

Author's Note

So... somewhere along the way I suggested that The Prankster Prince would have about seven books.

Well, clearly Thony (or maybe it was Amanita... or Dae... never count out Dae) pulled a prank on me, because that is clearly not happening.

I should have guessed. I mean, Thony just turned fifteen and his goal was not to find a princess-bride immediately, but rather to grow up a bit before he had to get married. And since it should have been obvious – with his attitudes and Amanita's attitudes – that Pathremir wasn't going to be a place he wanted to stay for very long... so that meant he was going to have to go off and have some more adventures...

Unfortunately, I'm sort of running out of kid/YA book series with formulaic titles to poke fun at.

So... I'm casting a bit farther afield.

Book Six is going to be A Court of Mists and Misadventures.

You can make some easy guesses about where Thony is heading... I mean, we already know that Queen Snowmistral (Puck's mom, the Queen of the Snow-Fairies... who are Mist-Maidens) wants to see him. The question might be if he makes it out of Queen Namarina's Court without causing more trouble for his friends than he wants to.

It's going to be out in March, so you'll just have to wait and see...

And I'm going to try to make it a little easier – here's a pre-order link for the eBook version of *A Court of Mists and Misadventures: Book Six of the Prankster Prince.*

https://tinyurl.com/Pre-Order-Prankster-Prince-6

(or use the QR code)

Have a great Holiday season – and maybe check out the other three books I have coming out in the next two months:

- *Double Down on Love,* an anthology of Kentuckiana romances featuring local authors, including award-winning and USA Today Bestselling authors (and me!). Available 11/29/24 in eBook (print soon ot follow), and all proceeds go to charity. Use this link to pre-order for only $2.99! https://tinyurl.com/DD-on-Love

- *The UnCaptive King: Book Five of the Chronicles of Ilseador,* also due out in NOVEMBER 2024. This book brings to a close the *Prydeen Prophecy Cycle...* but not the story of King Damien, Queen Genevieve, Adam and Jason.

- *Scaredy Cat: A Knightess of the Realm Holiday Prequel Novella,* due out in DECEMBER 2024. Ever wonder what the somewhat infamous Devin Metreedi was like – from his perspective? How about as the harried stay-at-home dad of three-year-old Karana? Like The Fall of Taridawil, which I put out last April, this book fills in some backstory. And – in case you're wondering – the 'holiday' referenced is Diwali, which Wave celebrates because of its large Pardasian expatriate population, and which is popular in Karana's family because Lord Andros' mother – who raised both him and Devin – was of Pardasian descent.

Happy reading!

Mangala

More Fantasy (and fiction) coming soon...

The UnCaptive King: Book 5 of the Chronicles of Ilseador
(available November 2024)

Double Down - A Kentuckiana Romance Writers Charity Anthology
(NOT fantasy)
(available November 2024)

Scaredy Cat (A Knightess of the Realm Holiday Prequel Novella)
(available December 2024)

An All-Too-Obvious Choice: Book 2 of the Secret of Dragon Mountain
(A Knightess of the Realm Novel)
(available January 2025)

About the Author

Mangala McNamara lives in Flyover Country (the far northern end of the US South) with her husband, The Professor, and four of her six children. The remaining children are in college – you can blame the oldest for the excessive amounts of math showing up in Mangala's fantasy novels, the second one for better attention to staging of scenes, the third for all the economics, and the fourth for great attention to history – and all of them for a focus on political science! Mangala is a former professional bellydance instructor, and used to enjoy knitting, crotchet and embroidering Temari balls but now is much more boring as she rarely does anything but write... although she also fences (the sport) and plays D&D with her kids. She owes her love of books and reading to her mother, who was a professional folklorist and could recite – from memory – stories from every nation in the United Nations.

Her **Knightess of the Realm** and **Chronicles of Ilseador** series occur in Amanita's homeworld.

Find out about Mangala's new projects and releases at
https://www.RisingDragonBooks.com

Also by Mangala McNamara

Fantasy in the World of the Living Gods:

The Prankster Prince
1. *Thony and the Much-Anticipated Adventure*

The Raven War (3 book mini-series)
2. *Thony Goes Astray! (in the Deep, Dark, and Dangerous Fairy Wood)*
3. *So You Want to Be a Hero?*
4. *How Thony Stopped a War (and Fixed a Friendship)*

Pathremiri Problems (2 book mini-series)
5. *Diary of a ~~RUNAWAY PRINCE~~ Bold Questing Hero*

Knightess of the Realm
   A Not-So-Sacrificial Maiden
   Out of the Woods… Hopefully (a Prequel Novella)
   The Fall of Taridawil (A Story Collection)

   The Heir's Journey mini-series (3 books)
       A Not-So-Simple Mission: Book One
       An Entirely-Unexpected Revelation: Book Two
       An All-Too-Surprising Homecoming: Book Three

   The Secret of Dragon Mountain mini-series
       An Altogether-Curious Altercation: Book One

The Chronicles of Ilseador
   The Rebel Duchess: Book One

   The Prydeen Prophecy Cycle mini-series (four books)
       The King's Champion: Book Two
       The Pirate-King: Book Three
       The Pale Sorceress: Book Four